# Keep Me in Mind

*Fixer upper meets found family in this new heartwarming small-town second chance romance when a matchmaking wedding planner reunites a lonely architect with the girl he promised to love forever.*

## LIAM

When my family moved across the country, I promised the only girl I've ever loved that I'd be back. To seal that promise and prove my love to her, I spent every last penny I earned on a promise ring.

But mere days later, the crushing blow of an email rocked my world—she'd decided not to wait for me, urging me to move on. When I returned to Palmer City later that year, I discovered she'd vanished into the foster care system after a tragic event at her home.

It's been nine years, and I've never given up hope of finding her. I've never let go of the dream that we could have a future together. When my cousin asks me to redesign our grandparents' old barn into a wedding venue, it's a no-brainer.

But when I show up for the job, it's *her* that my cousin hired to lead the construction. She's moved back to town, and all of the feelings I'd long-since buried have resurfaced—along with the dream I'd never truly given up on.

## BECK

Stunned. Shocked. Stupefied.

When I arrive at the barn to meet with the architect, the last thing I expect is to come face-to-face with the boy who promised to love me forever. The very same boy who had given me a promise ring, a long-lost symbol of his unwavering love and commitment. But even though I broke his heart, I could never quite let go of the love I had for him.

When our eyes lock, the buried feelings I had for him rush back. While hope and happiness fill his expression, my inner turmoil makes me want to bolt.

He doesn't deserve the mess that is me or the destruction I leave in my wake. I need to keep my distance, because if we fall in love again—as grownups—I know the heartache will be unbearable. I can't survive losing him again.

*This is a sweet return-to-hometown he-falls-first (again!) second chance wedding romance with heartwarming characters, found family, and even a matchmaking horse named Swiftie.*

*Author's Note: This book features characters from my Palmer City world. It's a stand-alone, but if you love the town and characters, be sure to check out my Palmer City Voltage series.*

# Keep Me in Mind

## BREWER BRIDES

## KERRY EVELYN

Swan Press

*To my Bridie Crew:*
*Andrea, Amanda K, Amanda P, Frieda, Hannah, Judy, Katie, Lori,*
*Sarah, Shanna, Tabitha, Tonya, and Valerie*

*Thanks for coming back to Palmer City with me!*

# A Note to Readers

Get exclusive access to all the Palmer City bonus content!
Read a free story and bonus epilogues, plus other fun freebies
like the Voltage roster and other printables when you sign up
for my newsletter at KerryEvelyn.com.

If you have a Spotify account, you can listen along to the
unofficial soundtrack as you read!
Tinyurl.com/BBKeepMeinMind

To my Palmer City Voltage readers, this story parallels the
timelines in *Christmas on Ice* through *Crushing on Ice*.

# A Note from Kerry

I'm so glad you've come to visit this charming old western town, where residents have been following their dreams for more than a century! In 1888, the Palmer and the Brewer families settled the land, dividing what would become a prosperous mining town into two equal parts. The details were decided by card games, and when the chips settled, the Brewers owned the land west of Snowpack creek, and the Palmers had control of everything east to the Colorado Springs border, as well as naming rights.

Over the years, the Palmer family began to dwindle, and in the '90s—the 1990s—Quinn Brewer and his wife, Angie, opened a sports bar and grill across from the new arena and mall—on the Palmer side of Snowpack Creek. Quinn's mother was a Palmer, and, well, the sale of that land is a story for another time!

With the addition of the arena, an all-in-one-stop sportsplex popped up on the west side, providing a place for professional athletes and townies alike to learn and play. Featuring pro hockey players to Olympic figure skaters to world-class all-star cheerleaders, the Plex rivals the Creek Walk on a Saturday night for the busiest place in town.

Local businesses along the creek are owned by the kindest and quirkiest residents this side of the Colorado River. Rock on a swinging creekside bench or stroll along Restaurant Row to the town park, a magical place to find love and solace in all the seasons. Everything is light and peaceful here in Palmer City ... mostly. With several new businesses popping up, including Quinn and Angie's daughter Brenna's wedding barn venue and a German-Italian fusion restaurant that'll be in direct competition with Brewski's, the laid-back residents of Palmer City are in for some unexpected drama.

*Return to Palmer City again and again*
*for all the Brewer Brides stories!*

✓ Second Chances (Keep Me in Mind) Liam & Beck
✓ Enemies-to-More (One Margarita) Keegan & Astoria
✓ Friends-to-More (Born to Fly) Lawson & Bailey
✓ Long-Time Love (Head Over Boots) Drew & Ellabee
✓ Marriage of Convenience ('Til You Can't) Alden & Anya
✓ Secret Pregnancy (Two Pink Lines) Jackson & Chelsea
✓ Workplace Romance (Make it Sweet) Brodie & Fyvie
✓ Girl/Guy Next-Door (Goodnight Kiss) Hayden & Brielle
✓ Stuck Together (Barn Song) Surprise Couple!

Plus
✔ Recurring Unforgettable Side Characters
✔ Found Family
✔ Small-Town Shenanigans
✔ Happily-Ever-Afters

For access to exclusive extra content, bonus epilogues, recipes, hockey rosters, printable activities and more, sign up for my newsletter at KerryEvelyn.com and join my group of VIP readers at Facebook.com/groups/CranesCoveCrew.

# Shining Star Barn Events
*Brenna's To-Do List*

**Who:** <u>Ranford-Brewer Wedding Squared</u>
**When:** <u>June</u>

## ~~12~~ 9 Months Before— *September*
  √ *Secure Venue*
  √ *Finalize business loan to renovate family barn*

## 8 Months Before— *October*
  √ *Hire architect*
  √ *Hire Contractor*

## 7 Months Before— *November*
  __ *Clear out barn*
  __ *Reunite Liam and Beck so they realize their HEA is with each other and add another happy couple to my Master Matchmaking File bwahaha*

<u>*Notes:*</u>
*\*Liam can't travel until Thanksgiving.*
*\*Beck's business license is still waiting on approval.*
*Vibe: Neither seem to feel the urgency (to get together). C'mon, people!*

# CHAPTER 1

## *Liam*

The first thing I saw when I slowed to a stop in front of my childhood home was the "For Sale" sign my cousin Brenna had told me about. I'd always said I wanted to live in that house forever, and now was my chance if I was serious about moving back.

The second thing I saw was that the house next door had been reduced to a pile of debris and ashes.

Brenna hadn't told me that Becky's house had burned down.

But then again, why would she? Becky and I hadn't spoken since—

*Nope.* Not gonna rehash that.

I parked my rental car in front of the neighbor's house across the street and gave a wave to old Mr. Palmer, who was on the roof hanging Christmas lights and sporting his signature ugly Christmas sweater. His red trucker hat was also covered in lights, and I couldn't help but grin.

It was good to see some things never changed. Judd and Maybelle Palmer weren't just our quirky former neighbors;

they were extended family. Every Thanksgiving morning since before I was born, he hung the lights while she prepared their family feast. Over the weekend, they'd set out the lawn decorations and giant inflatable characters.

They even had a working kid-size Ferris wheel with three gondolas. That had been the first year he'd won the town's "Best Light Display" award. Who could compete with that? Over the years, they added a skating pond, an elves' workshop, and even a child-size cottage where on weekend nights Mrs. Palmer distributed hot chocolate and Mr. Palmer dressed as Santa and handed out candy canes while littles played inside so their parents could stroll and steal smooches in the illuminated backyard maze.

The Ferris wheel had been my favorite, though. We kids had watched him build it, and he even let me help him paint it. On the first ride, I'd kissed Becky on her cheek for the first time when we reached the "top"—all of six feet in the air.

I exited the car and crossed the street to take a closer look at the sign on the lawn. A quick swipe on my phone brought up the listing. I knew it by heart since I'd looked it up a million times. This house was full of happy memories. I *did* want to live here again. But I'd always imagined living here with Becky. If I bought the house and moved back here from Rhode Island, would the ghost of her and what we once had haunt me?

Becky wasn't dead in the physical realm, but she'd ghosted *me* shortly after I professed my forever love to her.

That had hurt.

I turned toward the remains of the house she grew up in before fate sent her overseas. Well, what was left of it. Caution tape, boarded-up windows on the ground floor, and support beams poking out of the frame painted a sad canvas. Charred odds and ends littered the yard. The air carried the scent of burned wood and ash. I felt terrible for the family, who'd lost everything.

As I rounded the corner, I glanced up at my old bedroom window, then over to the spot where Becky's window used to be. The old maple next to her window hadn't been spared, either. In my mind, the image of a kindergarten Becky appeared, opening the window and stepping out onto the closest branch, desperate to escape her father's yelling, carefully climbing onto the limbs that led higher up. Though unsteady and stepping on her long princess nightgown twice, she was able to catch herself each time. I could only hold my breath and pray she didn't fall.

She stumbled less each time. Once, I got brave and opened my window, telling her she could come play Ninja Turtles with me if she could navigate over. She weaved her way in and out of the branches effortlessly. I was instantly in love. Any girl who could climb trees like that—and liked the Ninja Turtles— was okay in my book. It didn't matter that we were only five years old.

I shook my head to clear the memory ... and blinked as a flash of light stung my eye. There was something in the ground by one of the tree's exposed roots.

I walked over to take a closer look. Maybe it was a coin. I could sure use a lucky penny right now.

Reaching the base of the tree, I squatted down and reached for the small item nestled in the ashes. I scooped it up and sucked in a shuddering breath.

It couldn't be.

But it was.

In my hand was the promise ring I saved every extra cent for. It took me a year and a half of working summers on my grandparents' ranch and as a golf caddy and busboy at a country club outside Providence. I'd earned enough to buy Becky a real diamond so that she knew how much I loved her and wanted to be with her forever. It was a small diamond, but it was real. I thought that would mean something.

How wrong I was. A few days after I gave it to her, she disappeared from my life.

I'd always wondered if she kept the ring. Now I knew she hadn't. She'd buried it, and with it, my dreams.

I stood slowly, pocketing the ring and fighting back tears. She wasn't worth crying over. I'd done plenty of that a long time ago.

I turned away and walked back toward my car. "Can I give you a hand?" I called up to Mr. Palmer.

"What, you think an old man like me can't hang his own lights?"

I grinned at his response, anticipating the familiar argument. Mr. Palmer would accept help, but only after assuring the person offering he could totally do it himself.

"Of course you can," I said, rolling up the sleeves of my sweater as I strolled to the ladder propped against the garage roof. "If I didn't ask, you know Gran would have my head."

He chuckled. Gran was his favorite cousin. She'd committed the ultimate crime in our little town of Palmer City by marrying a Brewer, and that Brewer happened to be his best friend. Over time, the feud between our two founding families cooled, and now there were more Brewers than Palmers in the town, even including the five of us that moved across the country.

"I do know that. Well, come on up here then and tell me what the Rhode Island branch of Brewers has been up to."

I scurried up the ladder and fell into easy conversation as we looped the strings of lights onto the hooks screwed into the trim. "Dad got another promotion. Mom's still teaching. Coming up on retirement but she says they'll have to make her leave."

"Sounds like the Milliken and Elise I know. And your brothers?"

"Lawson graduated from college and is flying for a small regional airline. Brodie's in his second year at Johnson & Wales. He's been baking and decorating cakes for Mom's friends' kids and grandkids. But I think chocolate is where he'll end up."

"Always had a knack for making sweets, that kid—and eating them." Mr. Palmer inspected our work. "Well, the outline is done. Now to bring up Santa and his sleigh. Appreciate the help."

"No problem." On the lawn, the old plastic Santa, sleigh, and reindeer were laid out. "How about I carry them up and you place them?" I offered.

"I like that plan," he agreed. "And how about you? Job going well?"

I hesitated. "It's fine."

He snorted. "Doesn't sound like it. Are you bored, stifled, or being taken advantage of?"

I considered his question. "Probably a mix of all of that. I'm really looking forward to redesigning Gran's old barn. Brenna has some great ideas, and I'm excited to get creative—and work on something that's not an office building."

"I can see that. And the goal is to have it done for your cousins' weddings in June?"

"Yeah. We should make that timeline, no problem."

"I've no doubt you will. When you set your mind to something, you stick to it and see it through. Even when there's adversity." He shook his head with a small smile. "I like to think you get that from your Palmer side. Just like your grandmother."

I returned his grin, and we got to work on Santa and the reindeer. I couldn't keep my head from looking across the street though, and he called me on it.

"Shame what happened over there," he said. I got the sense his comment was double-edged; referring to the time Becky lived there, and the recent fire.

"Yeah," I agreed, handing up the last reindeer. "So much sadness in one place."

"Unsafe connections often lead to fire. Time for someone to rebuild and start over. Clean slate, once the past is bulldozed over."

He gave me lot to think about. Mr. Palmer often spoke in riddles, even when we were kids. What he didn't say was usually the point he was trying to make. He referenced the electrical fire that took out the home, but it made me think about the unsafe environment Becky grew up in.

When we finished, I returned to my car and drove to Brewski's for the annual friends and family Thanksgiving. My Uncle Quinn and Aunt Angie, the owners, hosted it every year for our family and out-of-town friends, including professional hockey players from the Voltage, the local minor league hockey team, who couldn't get home for the weekend. I'd grown up dining with hockey players, some of whom went on to play pro, and hanging out with them after my own games.

I reached into my pocket to make sure the ring was still there, and with one final look at my childhood home and the site of destruction next to it, I left it in my rearview.

It didn't matter that I hadn't been driving yet when we moved to Rhode Island. I knew the streets of Palmer City like the back of my hand. Becky and I had biked everywhere, sometimes with my brothers, sometimes just us. Once out of the neighborhood, there were two ways to get to Brewski's. I could take a shortcut through what was left of the Brewer ranchland through my grandparents' property, or cut through the downtown area and follow the creek north along Main Street.

Remembering my cousin Keegan had recently moved into a caboose he'd been restoring since last summer, I opted for the family land route. When the old train car came into sight, I wasn't disappointed. A grin spread on my face as I took in the dark green vehicle, trimmed in red and covered in strings of LED lights. In the surrounding space, makeshift Christmas trees composed of poles of various heights rose up from the ground, anchored in a circle by more strings of lights.

Keegan loved Christmas and was teaching himself to sequence lights to music. I'd need to come back at night to see his display lit up to its full glory.

*Becky would love this.* The thought crept in before I could stop it. When we were kids, her family didn't do much to celebrate aside from a few gifts on Christmas morning. Our family took the holiday to a whole other level, and she'd been a part of our crazy traditions until we moved away. The joy that lit up her face ... How could I *not* have fallen in love with her?

My grandparents' farmhouse looked the same as always. Icicle lights hung from the roof, gables, and porch. My parents and I and my younger brothers stayed there every Christmas. I'd opted to stay at the Creekside Inn downtown for this trip so I could work. My goal was to leave Brenna with a sketch and proposal by Sunday night, including a task list for Montoya Construction, a new veteran-owned contractor in town.

If I stayed with Gran and Gramps, I'd be sucked into family, favorite foods, and fun. *This was a working weekend,* I reminded myself.

I glanced at the car's digital clock as the barn came into view. Flashbacks filled my mind and made my face heat. How was I going to work here without going crazy? Almost every memory had Becky attached to it. Learning to ride, bottle-feeding a foal that almost didn't make it, playing Tarzan in the hayloft, our first *real kiss* …

Gran's horses had been moved to the other end of the property when Brewski's got busy. All the traffic had made them nervous. Except for Swiftie, the foal that Becky and I spent our entire summer nursing. The horse's mother had died shortly after birthing due to complications, and there hadn't been much hope for the baby. But Becky and I refused to give up on him.

Brewski's was hopping when I arrived. The sports bar and grill was also part brewery. Uncle Quinn had dabbled over the years with craft brews, and Keegan had picked up the hobby. The equipment lined the left side wall, and I found my family at the booths along the right-side wall. The center and bar were filled to capacity with friends and professional athletes and their families.

I recognized a few of the players from when my cousin Kingston played for the team. He'd been traded to the new expansion team, the Montana Mavericks, last summer. Everyone missed him in Palmer City, but they were so proud of him for leveling up and living his dream. All of us Brewer cousins had played hockey when we were kids, but only Kingston and my brother Lawson dreamed of a professional career. And of the two, only Kingston made it to the pros.

Aunt Angie was at the host stand with her back turned to the door. "Got room for one more?" I asked, sneaking up behind her.

She whirled around, a wide smile spreading on her face as she recognized me. "William Brewer! Of course!" She pulled me in for a hug and patted my back. "It's been, what, ten years since you've been here for Thanksgiving?"

"Nine, but who's counting?" I replied. Our family came up every Christmas, but due to school and hockey and dad's job, we'd never been able to make it back for the Thanksgiving holiday.

She clucked her tongue. "Still fast with the math, I see. You make sure you charge Brenna full price for your designs. No family discount." She leaned in closer. "Your Aunt Patricia and her doctor friends put up a hefty sum to finance this project. No cutting corners, no spared expense, got it?"

"Got it." That was a relief to hear. My colleagues at the Providence firm were already envious of my side job. Most of the projects we were hired for limited our expenses and creativity. I knew Brenna had some grand visions, and I would do everything I could to realize them.

A project like this in my portfolio would open me up to another level of work and allow me to be based anywhere. I'd been thinking about moving back here for some time now. New England was great and all, but it never felt like home.

"Brenna saved you a seat next to Keegan. See if you can get him to stay for dessert. I can tell he's already itching to head back to the safety and solitude of his office."

"Yes, ma'am." The eldest of us Brewer cousins, Keegan was mostly antisocial, but ask him about brewing or Christmas lights, and he'd talk your ear off. "And thank you for having me."

"It's our pleasure," she said, meeting my gaze with shining eyes. "We miss you all so much. The family still feels incomplete without you and your brothers here."

A lump formed in my throat. "I know the feeling."

She hugged me again, and I headed to my seat, again wondering again if it was time to move back. Palmer City had been, and always would be, my home.

Even without Becky.

## CHAPTER 2
### *Beck*

The day after Thanksgiving, I walked in the Brewer family barn feeling more like the old Becky than Beck. I needed to remind myself I wasn't that girl anymore.

I took a deep pull of the crisp November air into my lungs and wished my dad was with me. We'd started this business together, but even with my years of experience, I was nervous.

Why was I nervous?

Oh yeah. 'Cause I'd be working with Willy Brewer's cousin Brenna on her dream barn. It shouldn't be a big deal. Willy lived in Rhode Island, and it'd been almost a decade since we were together. He'd never come back west for Thanksgiving that I knew about, and I was pretty sure Black Friday was a work day for architects. There was no way he'd be here today.

So why was I sweating?

The barn door cracked open to reveal my childhood friend. Her long blond hair cascaded in waves over her shoulder and bounced when she squealed. "Becky! I mean Beck!"

"Hey, Brenna." I smiled shyly. *This is awkward.* She opened her arms for a hug, and we embraced.

"I'm so glad you're back. It was such a nice surprise running into you at the Bevvie Bar."

I forced a tight-lipped smile. *Surprise* had been an understatement. I'd tried to hide behind my dad so she wouldn't notice me, but then Dad pointed out the likeliness of running into her and other Brewers was inevitable, so I'd squared my shoulders and decided to face her head-on.

It's not that I didn't like her. I'd *loved* her as kid. She'd been the closest thing to a sister I'd had when Willy and his family lived here. Then he moved, she joined the high school cheerleading team, and we only saw each other in our shared classes. Which was fine, because it wasn't like I could have had any friends over to my house.

I shuddered at the thought.

"It's great to be back, mostly. I like being able to see Mom every day." I forced a smile. If this job went well and brought in steady work by word of mouth, I'd be able to afford the new surgery that might help Mom walk again.

Brenna frowned and squeezed me into another hug. "You must have missed her so much, living overseas for so long."

I thought about the long years living on the army base in Germany, and tears stung at the back of my eyes. I stepped out of her embrace before they could fall. "More than I can put to words." My reply came out husky, and I quickly turned my head and gestured to the expansive indoor space. I needed to focus on why I was here, in the barn, not my reasons for returning to Palmer City. "So, tell me your vision for this space."

Brenna's phone trilled, and she held up a finger. "Hold that thought for just a sec." She lifted the phone to her ear and walked back toward the open barn door. "Yes, I'm here. Just come right in."

A shadowy figure appeared in the space. About as tall as my dad but less bulky and—I gasped.

"*Willy?*" I whispered incredulously.

It couldn't be him. No way, no how. He wasn't supposed to be here.

But he was. The boy who'd been my best friend and then my boyfriend. The boy who ate all my tomatoes and welcomed me into his home, offering me the family life I'd only read of in books. The boy who asked me to wait for him and promised to love me forever.

As he stepped into view, I was sure of it. The lanky teen with the endearing crooked grin and nerdy glasses had grown into the most handsome man I'd ever seen in my life.

He still wore glasses, but they were thin and wire-rimmed, the same steely gray as his kind eyes. His short, trimmed beard was more of a five o'clock shadow that framed the features that haunted my sleepless nights. And though he was wearing a coat, it was evident he'd filled out his six-foot-two frame and wide shoulders.

Desperately, I scanned for something I could hide behind, as if that was viable option. My heart pounded against my ribcage in a rhythm that was surely dangerous for human survival. Hiding used to be my thing, but I was a grownup now. A businesswoman.

I could run. The back door was a straight shot from where I was standing.

*Stop it. Face him like a woman!*

If this hadn't been our first big job stateside, I would have.

But Dad and I needed Brenna's contract to build our business. Renovating this barn would showcase all our skills and artistry, and I was confident it'd lead to more jobs than we could handle—if it went well. We wanted to be based close to Mom.

Maybe Willy wouldn't recognize me. My hair was shorter and straighter, and I wore glasses now.

He stepped inside before I could bolt. Brenna chatted in his ear, then gestured my way. His gaze met mine, and he froze.

Oh yeah, he *definitely* knew who I was.

Brenna grinned so mischievously I had to wonder if she'd set us up to work together on purpose. "Beck, you remember my cousin Liam, right?"

*Liam?* I gave a curt nod, but no sound came out when I opened my mouth to greet him.

This job was going nowhere if neither of us could speak.

I tried again. "Hi."

He blinked, and his arms rose to cross over the front of his chest, as if to protect his heart. I couldn't blame him.

He tipped his chin in greeting.

Ever the peacemaker, Brenna grinned wider and looped her arm through his, almost knocking him over since his arms were so tightly pressed to his chest. I willed my feet to plant themselves in place as I realized she was dragging him toward me.

I took a step back—straight into a beam. I jumped forward, right into Brenna's path. Caught, she looped her free arm around my waist and held tight.

*Well.* This was awkward.

"Look around, you two. Can you see it? The rafters polished and stained in their natural color, wispy draped tulle everywhere, elegant chandeliers and tables set with candles inside hurricane sconces. A dais under the loft and a path of white carpet down the center, flowers everywhere ... Will it work, Liam?"

The structure of the barn looked sound, but all I saw in the moment was old rusted farm equipment and a half dozen horse stalls I itched to demolish. I wondered how soon I could start destroying the interior.

I turned my head to look up at Brenna. Her eyes were closed, and a dreamy expression lit up her face. Liam stared straight ahead, tight-lipped, eyebrows raised thoughtfully.

"The potential is here," he said finally, in a rich low timber that was far from the youthful teen boy voice that still spoke to me in my dreams. I nearly swooned. "If we can get it cleared out by tomorrow night, I can assess the structure and work up a sketch on Sunday. It's going to take a bigger crew than just us three, though."

"My dad will help," I said. "He's visiting Mom today, but he'll be here tomorrow."

Liam's expression hardened. "No. That guy almost killed your mom. Isn't he in jail?"

I rushed to explain. It hadn't occurred to me that he didn't know the full story of what really happened all those years ago. "Not who you think is my dad. That guy *is* in jail. My *real* dad. The one Mom never told me about until her accident."

His eyes widened, and he stepped away from Brenna. "Your *real* dad?"

Brenna patted him on his shoulder. "I'm going to head over to Brewski's and see who I can round up for tomorrow." Her gaze darted nervously between us. "You two should, um, catch up." She gave my waist a squeeze and hurried out of the barn.

Classic setup, and I fell for it. I leaned back against the beam and sighed. Bringing up those old memories would be agonizing. And I had a good feeling Liam would be even more upset with me for pushing him away when he learned the truth.

# CHAPTER 3

*Liam*

N *ot her real dad?* She'd called him "Dad." Maybe the fact that Dirk Monroe wasn't her father explained why he hadn't cared a lick about her growing up, except to scream at her when she fell short of his impossibly high standards—or if she breathed wrong.

And I hated that her mother brushed it off or blamed it on Becky's being born early, like she wasn't smart because her brain didn't develop properly. Becky was the smartest girl I knew. And Dirk Monroe was an abuser and the kind of father other kids had nightmares about and thanked God that he wasn't theirs. He didn't deserve to be a dad.

Becky slid down the beam to the dirt floor and pulled her knees into her chest. "It's a long story, Willy," she said softly, averting her aquamarine eyes that had so often been filled with pain. "I don't want to talk about it."

I nodded again. I wanted her to tell me everything, but only if—or when—she was ready to. I felt a primal urge to rip away the blanket of pain that had settled upon us, cocooning us in memories we both wished to forget.

"Okay," I said. I wouldn't push. "I go by Liam now." I cringed as she met my gaze with a frown. That sounded pompous.

I needed to explain. Lowering myself to the floor, I mirrored her position. "That summer we moved ... the first day at the new rink for hockey camp, I introduced myself as Willy and the other kids lost it and said I'd be bullied mercilessly. So they decided an intervention was in order, and I went with it. New guy in town, new name, new me. It stuck. I never told you because I liked that you were the only one left that called me Willy. It meant something to me."

She nodded and lifted her gaze to meet mine. "I get it. I go by Beck now. That's what Dad—my real dad—calls me, and it's easier to get construction leads with a more masculine name." Her lip turned up at the corner in a half smile, and much like when we were younger, I wanted to do or say something to earn a full one. Becky's childhood had not been a happy one, but when she'd been with me and my family, she seemed lighter.

"So ..." I recalled the link to the website Brenna had sent me, listing the names of the contractors. "Beck Montoya?" I asked. "Your real dad's last name? Or your husband?" I did my best to feign ignorance. I had a good feeling Brenna wouldn't have set us up like this if Becky wasn't single.

She giggled, and there it was. *That* smile. The tension lifted immediately, and I relaxed.

"I'm not married." She held up her hand. "No ring, see?" Then her eyes widened, and she hung her head again.

I knew exactly what she was thinking about, but I didn't want to ruin the moment. Ignoring the elephant in the barn, I held my own left hand up and wiggled my fingers. "Me either. See?"

Beck raised her head again, and I read the relief in her eyes.

"Tell me about him," I prompted.

She smiled. "His name is Estéban Montoya. Before Mom lost the ability to speak—we think that happened in transport after her accident, because she was able to talk after she fell down the stairs—she told me to find my real dad. He was in the army and didn't know about me."

"Oh wow." Dirk the Jerk wasn't her real dad? I wondered what reason her mother had for keeping that secret for seventeen years. "And he's a good guy?" I had to make sure.

There was the smile again. Wide and toothy and I couldn't take my eyes off it. I found myself smiling back.

"Yeah. The best kind of dad. Like yours." She pushed her glasses up her nose in the most adorable way someone could execute such a thing. "After I spent a few weeks in foster care, they found him stationed in Germany. I changed my last name to his, finished high school there, and attended online college while working on the base. We started a renovation business and worked on projects when Dad was off duty."

"Foster care? I didn't hear about that part." It sounded traumatizing. Instinctively, I reached out but pulled my hand back.

She closed her eyes. "I didn't have anywhere else to go. But it wasn't for long. The hardest part was deciding what to bring with me."

I felt like I couldn't breathe. Becky had gone through all this while I was at the airport, completely unaware. "I'm so sorry. I can't imagine having to decide all that, plus worrying about your mom and learning your dad—stepdad—was a monster. What happened to all your stuff?"

She opened her eyes and gave a small smile. "The Palmers packed it up and put it in storage. Every time Dad brought me back to visit, we went through some things and took pictures so Mom could decide what she wanted to keep, too."

"Wow. And—now you're here to stay?" I thought Brenna had said she was, but I wanted to hear it from Becky's lips.

"Yes. Last summer, Dad retired from the army, and we made plans to move to Colorado. We both wanted to come out here to be with Mom—he'd forgiven her for not telling him about me, and he knew how much I missed her. So we found a rental close to the creek and moved in a few weeks ago. I ran into Brenna at the Bevvie Bar, and here we are now."

"Here we are now," I repeated. I took a deep breath and held out my hand. "Beck Montoya, pleased to make your acquaintance. I'm Liam Brewer."

She placed her hand in mine, and a shock jolted us both. "Call me Becky," she said huskily, her gaze meeting mine.

Instead of shaking her hand, I squeezed it gently. "It's a pleasure to meet you, Becky," I said, as if she wasn't the girl that broke my heart and buried the pieces in her side yard. "You can call me Willy, if you want."

She squeezed my hand back, more tightly than I was expecting, and stared intensely into my eyes. "I'd like that."

There was so much more in that gaze. And I wanted to know all of it.

TABBI AND DANNY WARNER, the owners of the Creekside Inn, ate breakfast with their granddaughters at 8 a.m. every weekend morning and invited guests to join them. Caitlyn, Madiella, Lorelai, and Hanna were ten, eight, six and four and were a big help on busy weekends. The girls' parents were former childhood stars from a kids' variety show and worked many weekends on the convention circuit, so the girls came over after school most Fridays and stayed until Sunday night. They loved to help their grandparents with chores and entertaining guests after dinner, often reenacting scenes from their favorite books and movies in the formal living room.

After an enjoyable breakfast of Belgian waffles and all the fixin's—including a mountain of whipped cream doled out by Lorelai—I arrived at the barn early Saturday morning, before Brenna and her volunteer crew, who were due just after noon. I wanted to get a better sense for the space, take some measurements, and refine some of my rough drawings before the crowd arrived.

I was sitting on the bench seat of the antique carriage frame working on the floor plan when a loud, tiny voice broke my concentration.

"Mr. Liam is here!"

I stood and turned as three-year-old Ryleigh Spencer, Brenna's BFF Kami's daughter, ran toward me at full speed, her pink Santa hat bobbing with each step. I'd met her yesterday at Thanksgiving and she was a ... *Handful* probably wasn't the best word. Capable, demanding, full of personality, and a bundle of fun didn't begin to describe her, though.

"Up!" she demanded when she reached me. I set my sketchbook down and reached for her before she could hurt herself, setting her gently on the seat next to me. The rusty, rickety frame was a tetanus nightmare waiting to happen. "Mr. Liam, why do you have a turkey on your bum?"

A turkey on my—

I groaned. No wonder Madiella and Lorelai were giggling at me as I left the breakfast table. I stood up again and reached around to my backside. I felt the sticker right away and peeled it free.

"Ryleigh!" Brenna rushed over. "You've got to be careful, sweetie. This barn isn't safe for little girls to run around in."

Ryleigh swung her legs and shrugged. "I'm careful. See? Mr. Liam helped." She thrust her hands out in front of her. "Go, horsey, go!"

Brenna shook her head, but she was smiling. "Good thing." She turned to me. "Trask will be here by one o'clock to pick her up, so we just have to keep her out of trouble until then." Trask Emerson played for the Voltage, and everyone knew he was sweet on Ryleigh's mom. He often babysat her when her father wasn't available so her mom could work.

"Did someone say trouble?" I looked toward the open doors as Brendan Trotter, Trask's defense partner, sauntered in. Kingston had lived with his family in Minnesota when he played junior hockey, and now Brendan had been picked up by the Voltage and was living in Kingston's apartment.

Funny how fate brought people into and out of each other's lives.

"Speaking of ..." Brenna murmured. She swallowed, and her cheeks reddened. That was interesting. I'd never seen her flustered like this.

"No trouble! Just me!" Ryleigh called.

"I thought Trouble was your middle name?" Brendan shot back.

Ryleigh giggled. "No, silly. Want to ride in my carriage? Mr. Liam, can you pretend to be the horsey?"

Brendan snorted as he approached us. "How 'bout we explore that space up there?" He pointed to the hayloft and bent toward her, speaking in a loud faux whisper. "I have a big secret idea, but I need to know if it's good or not before I tell Brenna. Will you listen and tell me if it's any good?"

"Oooh!" Ryleigh squealed and clapped her hands. "Let's go!"

Brendan reached for her, and she jumped into his arms. When they were out of earshot, I raised an eyebrow at my cousin. "Secret idea?"

She shrugged. "No clue." She turned toward the doors. "The crew should be here any minute. I thought I'd come a little early to see if you had any questions before we clear it out?"

I shook my head. "No. Just a little sad to see it like this. We had so much fun here as kids. A lot of memories."

"Yeah." She smiled. "I miss the horses being here."

A particular memory panged my heart. "Gran is still riding Swiftie?" Becky and I had nursed the horse just a few feet from where I was sitting. He'd survived and grown up to be my grandmother's favorite.

Brenna grinned. "Yup. And he still dances and prances to Taylor Swift songs."

I laughed as I slid down from the bench seat. Becky had been obsessed with the singer and played her music twenty-four seven. Gran said I could name the horse, and I had every intention of naming him Michelangelo until I thought about naming the horse after Becky's favorite fandom. It succeeded in impressing her, and I'll never forget how her expression lit up like a Christmas tree.

That was the summer I fell in love with her. We went from being best friends to more when I asked if I could kiss her—not on the cheek—in the very hayloft Brendan was exploring with Ryleigh.

Before I could change the subject to push the memory away, Becky and her dad arrived. She resembled the tall veteran in every way but stature: dark wavy hair, tan skin, eyes the color of the aquamarines you could still find in the local gem mines. But she was short like her mom, five-foot-three in her steel-toed work boots at most.

"So you're Wil-liam " he said, offering his hand. He spoke in a gentle, rhythmic accent that immediately put me at ease. "Estéban Montoya. Please, convey my thanks to your family for their kindness to my girl."

I swallowed and returned his firm grip, darting a glance to Becky. "Of course. It's an honor to meet you, sir."

He nodded and turned to Brenna, who waved Brendan over from the base of the ladder with Ryleigh in his arms. "Thanks for choosing us for the job. What's the plan?"

"Here's what I've got so far," I said, holding out the sketch pad and using my mechanical pencil to point to the features. "Most of this will be open space. Hardwood flooring stained to match the beams from the front doors to the back of the dais, which will be centered under the loft. Behind it will be the restrooms. A spiral iron staircase will replace the ladder to the loft. Large chandeliers down the center aisle here, here, and here, and smaller ones on each side. Bar area here, with full power and water hookups, plus refrigeration for kegs and bottles. Office upstairs—'

"And an apartment up there for Auntie Brenna!" Ryleigh and Brendan joined our little circle, and she pointed to the loft.

"An apartment?" I asked.

"You know Brenna," Brendan interjected. "She'll eat and sleep here 'til a job is done. There's enough space for a kitchenette, closet, and sleeper sofa, which can double as client seating. I can show you—"

"Later." Brenna held up a hand to cut him off and met my confused gaze. "He's right about that. Do we have enough in the budget for it?"

I glanced up at the loft and did some mental calculations. "Shouldn't be a problem. It's a good idea. It'll require extra time and materials, though, but your mom insisted we spare no expense."

"We can do it," Becky assured us.

"Great," Brenna said. "I'm so excited!"

I finished explaining the plan as the clear-out crew began to arrive. Brenna delegated jobs to family members and Brendan's teammates, and we spent the rest of the day clearing the space. A few times, I caught Becky looking over at me. Each time, I'd catch her gaze and smile. There was pain behind her eyes, and I wanted more than anything to right all the wrongs and make her happy again.

At least, as happy as she used to be. Before she dumped me via email and shattered my heart.

CHAPTER 4

## *Beck*

Once our plan was settled, I gathered the crew. "Brendan, split up your guys. Half can go with Dad to break down the horse stalls, and the rest can clear out all the old hay and equipment." I turned to Brenna. "Willy and I will go up to the loft and check out the space. Let us know if you have any special requests."

It felt almost too private to call him Willy in public. After more than a few conspiratorial winks from Brenna, I'd had enough.

He followed me up the ladder and to the back of the space. Memories flooded back, and from the wistful look on his face, I could assume he was also walking down memory lane. "Maybe … we should save Becky and Willy for when we're alone?"

"You want to be alone with me?" he teased, and it was as if no time had passed.

I frowned. I couldn't lose my heart to him again. "Or maybe not at all. It's probably a bad idea to get too personal. This is an important job for me."

His eyes narrowed. "It's important to me, too.'

"I didn't mean it wasn't—"

"I know." He sighed. "All right. *Beck.*" He emphasized the "kuh," and I winced. It sounded unnatural, but it was for the best.

"Thanks, *Lee-um.*" I swallowed. That felt awkward.

"So." He gestured to the back wall. "I'm thinking a big window here. Desk area to the right with bookshelves lining the wall behind it. To the left, a living area with a kitchenette. Piping will connect to the restrooms below."

"Sounds good. It looks like there's enough space to close it off and make a balcony, like in Brendan's sketch. It'd be tacky if wedding guests had a view of Brenna's office space."

He walked toe-to-toe from the back wall to the edge of the loft. "It'll be tight and cut into her space considerably, but I see your point."

We discussed a few more details and headed back down the ladder. Liam (it would take a while for me to get my head straight calling him that) insisted on going down first, in case I tripped.

"I'm not as klutzy as I used to be, you know," I said as I stepped off the ladder onto the dirt floor. "A few mishaps with heavy equipment cured me of that."

I laughed at his concerned expression and turned toward the door as a familiar whinny echoed into the barn.

"Swiftie!" I hurried across the space and outside to greet the white-and-gray dappled horse. Perched atop him, Liam's grandmother waved.

"Becky! You've been in town for weeks and haven't been by. Ol' Swiftie was a bit brokenhearted about that, so I decided to ride out so you could assure him he's still your favorite."

I laughed and reached up to pet Swiftie's neck. After a quick sniff, he was nuzzling me like no time had passed.

Mrs. Brewer dismounted and held up a few sugar cubes. "Trade you these for a hug."

I almost cried. She and her husband had been the closest things that I'd ever had to grandparents. My mother's parents had died when I was young, my stepdad had become estranged from his, and my real dad's folks were in New Mexico. I'd met them a few times, but we didn't have much of a relationship.

Yet. I hoped that would change now that we lived on the same continent.

It felt amazing being held, and though I tried, I couldn't stop the tears from escaping. "I'm sorry. For everything."

She held me at arm's length and lifted her hand to brush a thumb over my cheek to wipe away the tears. "Don't apologize. You've been through more than any kid should ever have to go through. I'm just glad you're back. Swiftie here is, too. Come on over anytime to say hi or take him for a ride. He's getting lazy."

"Thank you." I smiled and looked over my shoulder, back into the barn. Liam was watching us from the doorway. "Want to meet my dad?" I asked her.

"You bet." She took my hands in hers and squeezed. "Lead the way."

The rest of the day passed in a blur, and twilight descended all too soon. The early sunset over the mountains was just as I'd remembered, and in the weeks we'd been back, I hadn't missed being outside to witness it once. I was standing in the field, watching the brilliant colors of the painted sky change from bright blues to warm orangey tones, when I felt Liam's presence behind me.

"I'm going to order Papa Raffino's for everyone," he said. "Still like Hawaiian, I hope?"

I nodded. "Yes, thank you."

A few moments passed. We stood there in silence as the remainder of light disappeared below the silhouette of mountains.

"I miss these sunsets so much," he confessed.

"Why did you never move back?" The question had been weighing heavily on my mind. I thought for sure he'd return after college, as he'd always planned.

"It didn't seem right after the rest of my plans fell through." *Ouch*. "And when I was offered a permanent position at the firm where I interned, it seemed like a sign to stay in Providence."

I nodded. "You like your job, then?"

He shrugged. "It's okay. It pays a lot. It's good experience. But it's not where I want to spend the duration of my career."

I chewed on my lower lip until I worked up the courage to ask him what I most wanted to know. "Do you ever think of moving back here?"

"Every day," he replied, meeting my gaze. "My old house is for sale."

I held my breath. I loved that house and always imagined living in it. I wonder if Dad and I—

Nah. It would be too painful. I could never live there without Willy.

*Liam.*

Neither of us spoke for a few minutes, but I'm sure we felt

what the other was thinking. If things had been different, we'd be putting in an offer on that house, together. I closed my eyes and allowed myself to dream for a few minutes. This time of year, we'd be sitting side by side on the porch swing, watching kids from around the neighborhood explore the Palmers' festive yard. Maybe even have a child or two of our own ...

"Um, I should go order the food," Liam said, his voice breaking into my daydream. "Is it okay if I text you if any issues arise or I have any questions while I'm working on the designs?"

I nodded. "Of course." He pulled out his phone, and I recited my number for him to tap into his contacts.

"Thanks," he said and turned to go. My phone buzzed in my pocket, and I pulled it out as he disappeared back into the barn.

I swiped to read the text.

> I'm glad to be working on this project with you. —Willy

# CHAPTER 5

## Liam

B ack in Providence, the December Doldrums set in, even before November had run out. Going into the office was a chore, working on the same type of boring office buildings I'd been designing for years irritated me to no end, and little things began to feel like big things.

"We're scrapping the bump-out bay windows on the Sundlun project," my boss announced, poking his head into my office. "I'll need an alternative design on my desk before the client meeting tomorrow, m'kay?"

I looked up from my drafting table, where I was putting the finishing touches on that exact project, and stared hard into his eyes. I'd have to work all night to get that done, which meant putting the barn project to the side.

"The client didn't like it?" I asked. I knew the opposite to be true. I'd gone to high school with Dr. Regina Sundlun and knew her personally. She'd specifically requested this particular feature for her pediatric patients to use as a reading nook while they waited for treatment.

"Something like that." He shrugged. "The bump-outs affect the bottom line."

*Ours or Dr. Sundlun's?* I wanted to ask.

"Have it on my desk by noon tomorrow." He pivoted on his heel before I could reply.

Fuming, I pulled out my phone to text Becky—er, Beck.

> Someth ng came up and I have to work tonight. Can we move our video chat to tomorrow? I don't think I'll be home by the time it gets dark in CO.

She replied right away.

> I can send pictures if you need them for tonight.

> I won't be able to work on the barn tonight. I have to overhaul a design for a lunchtime client meeting tomorrow.

> Oh okay. Tomorrow works then. Same time?

> Yeah. Thank you. Any new developments?

I asked her that same question every day.

Permitting came through this morning. Just waiting on our license now to get started. Should be any day. Dad and I are keeping busy with handyman requests and hanging Christmas lights. We could probably work eighty hours a week at that. When we posted to the community group pages, I couldn't even imagine so many residents of Palmer City and Elk Creek Falls would want such a service.

I smiled, imagining Beck and her dad working together to light up our town and the one just north of us.

Be careful on those ladders. I'd be sad if anything happened to my favorite contractor.

I hit the send button before I could think twice about calling her my favorite. Thinking about her and the way we used to be, long ago, crept to the front of my mind more often than I'd expected. And of course, her safety weighed on my mind. I wasn't sure if I believed she'd lost all her klutziness. Becky had always fallen and picked herself back up when we were kids, assuring me she was fine—even when she wasn't.

I could say the same for you. Try not to stress so much, okay?

If only.

As I PREDICTED, Dr. Sundlun wasn't happy with the proposed changes, and by one o'clock my original designs were in her hands. The company was lucky she hadn't fired us. My busywork from the previous day was discarded, and I once again found myself questioning my future at the firm—and in Rhode Island.

My old house was still on the market. I swiped through the listing's pictures on my phone. The house had been decorated for fall when it'd been photographed. Leafy, colorful wreaths adorned the double front doors. A scarecrow held court in the front garden. Three shades of chrysanthemums hung in pots on the porch. Deep brown and mustard throw pillows decorated the sectional sofa. An oil painting of leaves changing colors hung on the wall above it with the quote "I'm so glad I live in a world where there are Octobers."

The kitchen and dining room were equally festive, staged with autumnal accents. The bedrooms were laid out in similar configurations as they'd been when I'd lived there and were surprisingly sparse for a family with what I assumed were three young girls, if one went by the canopied princess-themed twin and toddler beds and a pink crib. The back porch faced west toward the mountains, and I again felt a stab of nostalgia as I studied the vista in the background.

Could I really buy the home? I could afford it, especially since the asking price had been reduced, no doubt due to the mess next door. It was a fair ask, so why hadn't it been snapped up? The lot was sizable, the neighborhood was one of the best, and it was ideally located.

Tuesday night, I arrived home just in time for my video chat with Becky. I swiped to answer as I let myself into my apartment.

"Willy? Are you there?"

A rush of warmth heated my cheeks at her gentle greeting.

"I'm here," I replied, hurrying to flick on the lights. *I'll always be here for you,* I wanted to say. "Sorry, I just got home."

"No worries. How are the plans coming?"

"Almost done. I spent some time on them before work this morning." I'd awakened from a dream just after 4 a.m. and by five, I realized I wasn't falling back asleep.

I strode over to my desk, set up perpendicularly to the large window that looked out over Water and Bridge Streets toward the Providence River. Around me, the city was lit up and bustling.

On the other side of my screen, the opposite was true. Virtual silence, *peaceful* silence surrounded Becky in the barn. I couldn't see outside, but I imagined the light growing paler and the stars awaiting their turn to light up the sky. The more I connected with her and my family in Palmer City, the more I missed that life.

It was almost painful. The pangs of homesickness were becoming increasingly distracting and troublesome. I'd need to find a cure before I went crazy.

"We're almost finished with the initial cleaning. Brendan and his teammate Xavier have been by a few times to help. The extra hands have put Dad and I ahead of schedule."

"That's great. You'll be ready to go as soon as all your paperwork comes in." I glanced at the tent-style calendar Mom had given me for Christmas last year. How many days until I could go back?

"That's the plan." She adjusted her glasses with a gloved hand.

I really liked her in glasses.

"I'm taking vacation," I blurted, surprising myself. "December thirteenth through January second." Good thing I still had three weeks left to use or lose. "I want to be there when you start. To help."

She sucked in a breath. "Okay."

*Okay?* Not quite the reaction I'd been hoping for, but she didn't object.

Distance was doing its number on me, making my heart grow fonder and such.

No, that wasn't true.

The way I felt about Becky—*Beck*—hadn't changed. I still loved her. I knew that deep in my gut. And I wanted her back. Somehow, I'd messed that up before.

So I'd tread lightly, measuredly. Put out feelers. Read her carefully, and plan strategically.

I couldn't shake the overwhelming truth that we were meant to be together. I just needed her to believe it, too.

# CHAPTER 6

## *Beck*

Willy—er, Liam would be arriving tomorrow, and it was throwing me off my game. After I hammered my thumb for the third time, Brenna suggested I take the rest of the day off. I took one long look at the pallets of insulation and decided it wouldn't set me too far behind if they weren't all installed in the loft this very moment.

Colorado winters were *cold*. Even though the sun shone more days in Denver than it did in Central Florida, the nights were downright frigid. Brendan had insisted Brenna forsake aesthetics for practicality in the living space above, and I agreed with him. It was an easy enough install, and we could stain the new wood covering it to match below.

Heating the open space below would be the real challenge. That would be a job for Liam and the HVAC team to figure out. Brenna was adamant that we keep the outer walls as is.

I decided to visit my mother at her assisted living facility, Mountainview Manor. I loved the drive there. It was off Stagecoach Road near the sportsplex, recreational fields, and Gretzky Pond. A beautiful area with a gorgeous view of the

Rockies, the sprawling campus had several buildings, each dedicated to a different level of care from independent living to a full-service nursing home. Mom's building, Colt House, served those who needed long-term care. Victims of accidents, veterans whose injuries prevented them from living along, and the like.

Peeking through the window on her door, I was happy to find my dad sitting beside her, him on the sofa and her in her wheelchair. My heart panged seeing her laugh while he spoke with immeasurable affection in his expression.

I watched them for a few moments, not wanting to interrupt and imagining what my life might have been like if he hadn't left—or if she'd told him she was pregnant. They'd gone to high school together outside Albuquerque and, from what I'd gleaned from Dad, were very much in love.

Yet she married my stepfather only two months after Dad left and never once tried to find him. He was older, had just graduated from college, and had a job waiting for him in Colorado Springs. We moved a few times until we settled into the house in Palmer City.

I don't remember much about those early years, only that he yelled a lot and I would hide. I didn't find out he was physically abusing Mom until I was a teenager, when I accidentally walked in on her in the bathroom, artfully applying makeup to a bruise on her upper jawbone, just below her ear. She made excuses, and I didn't push.

I wished I had listened to my gut and told someone. If I had, she wouldn't be paralyzed and mute.

Mom was scribbling something on the handheld whiteboard she used to communicate. Dad leaned over to read it, then threw his head back and laughed, catching me looking on as he opened his eyes. His smile broadened, and he made a waving gesture for me to enter.

Slowly, I opened the door and crossed the room. "Hey, Mom," I said, leaning down to hug her. She kissed my cheek and squeezed me tight.

Dad slid over and patted the cushion nearest the wheelchair. I sat down gratefully. He was kind, considerate, loving—everything my stepdad hadn't been.

"I was just telling your mom about the job we did at the Schwann castle. Do you still have pictures on your phone?"

"I do." I found the album quickly and handed the phone to Mom. "We spent two weeks there turning the master suite into an accessible apartment. The old man who owns it is in his eighties and becoming increasingly less mobile. Isn't it beautiful?"

Mom nodded as she slowly swiped. When she finished, she gave the phone back to me and picked up her whiteboard to write. I scooted closer to read while she scrawled.

*What a beautiful place! That must have been an incredible experience.*

"It was," I affirmed. "The Schwanns are descended from noble families, and parts of the castle have been closed off for years. They have a plan to fix it up over the next few years and leave it to their kids and grandkids as a vacation home."

*Will you go back to Europe to work on it?*

I shook my head. "No. It was during that job I felt the most homesick. His whole family came to visit one of the weeks we were there." I reached over to hold her hand. "I was overwhelmed with a fierce homesickness, missing you."

Tears welled in her eyes, and she squeezed my hand, then let go, picking up her board again. *I'm so glad you're both here.*

"I know," I whispered.

My phone buzzed on the cushion where I'd left it. Liam's name flashed at the top of the screen before disappearing.

"Do you need to check that?" Dad asked.

"Not really," I said, but my gaze didn't lift from the screen.

"But you want to," he teased softly.

My cheeks heated. "I plead the fifth."

He chuckled, and I looked up to find Mom smiling at me.

"Fine, I'll read it," I huffed. I picked up the phone and swiped to my text messages.

> I changed my flight to arrive earlier in the day. Would you like to review the plans over dinner?

I sucked in a breath as my heartbeat quickened. I was sure my face had gone from pink to red to purple in the last few seconds by the way my parents were staring at me. Was he asking me on a date?

Nah. This was strictly business. He didn't want to waste a minute of his trip, and by meeting the night before the first full day of work, we'd be saving time. Besides, why would he want to date me after I dumped him so cruelly and completely?

Simple answer: He wouldn't.

So why did that realization fill me with disappointment?

# CHAPTER 7

# *Liam*

After a final glance in the mirror, I cautiously opened the door and stepped out onto the veranda outside my suite. No sign of the Warner girls. I didn't mind their pranks, but they kept me on my toes and taught me to be cautious. The Olde Train Station Ristorante and Lounge was a short walk up the creek from the inn. Though I wanted to pick Becky up at her house, I suggested meeting her there instead.

Best to keep it casual.

Ha. The restaurant was anything but. When the mining in the town died out, so did the need for an out-of-the-way train stop. Decades ago, it was converted into a boutique hotel and featured a high-end restaurant on the ground floor—too fancy for every day, so most townies saved it for special occasions. However, it was the only place in town where we weren't likely to run into anyone we knew. Namely, a Brewer.

My relatives were everywhere.

And, for me, this *was* a special occasion.

When I made the reservation, I explained my need for a

large table and privacy. Important business meeting, I'd emphasized.

Every word was true. Becky was my most important business.

From my vantage point in the back corner of the main dining room, I had a clear view of the entrance. I was glad I'd arrived early to sit and settle my nerves. Knowing Becky, she'd likely also be early.

And she was. I couldn't take my eyes off her as the hostess led her toward me. A thin, glittery headband held her hair back from her face, which was in full view without her glasses. Her tan cheeks held a hint of pink from the blustery night, and her lips were colored in a tinted red gloss. Beneath her hip-length jacket, a dark green skirt teased bare knees peeking out above high brown boots.

It took every ounce of restraint not to jump up and help her remove her coat and pull out her chair. Instead, I held a cool smile—not too big, not too small—while she peeled off her coat, revealing a form-fitting cable-knit sweater dress.

It was a good thing she spoke first, because I seemed to have lost my voice.

"This place hasn't changed much," she remarked, settling into her chair. "Does your family still come here for your mom's birthday?"

She remembered.

"We do." My mother's birthday was the day after Christmas, so we were always in town for it. We'd always invited Becky. Some years she was allowed to come; other years her father—stepfather—would say no for no good reason.

My gaze flickered to the unopened menus. We always shared the Tour of Italy. She loved lasagna, I loved their spaghetti and meatballs, and we split the stuffed manicotti shells. On the years she hadn't come, I still ordered it and brought her the leftovers.

Until she disappeared.

I cleared my throat. "I thought we could have some privacy back here."

She gave a cursory glance to her left and right. "Good plan. Monday night crowd is thin, and all the football fans are probably at Brewski's or Paddy Maroon's."

I nodded. The server came by to take our drink order, and I moved over to the empty chair next to me to unroll the blueprints on the section of table that had been left clear. I turned them to face Becky.

"Oh, wow." She lightly ran her finger along the section of loft space. "Has Brenna seen these yet?"

I shook my head. "I wanted your thoughts first. There's no point in showing her something that's not finalized."

"I don't know what else you would add to this." She looked up and met my gaze. "It's got everything she's asked for, and the plan is detailed to the point where I can't think of a single question." She pointed to the center of the blueprint. "Phase 1, Structural. Support beams, restrooms, plumbing." Her finger slid to the exterior wall. "Phase 2, Woodwork. Staining, polishing, flooring. Then the loft. It even takes feng shui into account."

I smiled. "I think it's important. Some might feel that it's silly, but there's a lot of value in living and working in spaces that serve you and feel secure."

Our gazes locked, and I knew we were both thinking of her childhood home, which was everything but.

*Stupid.* Why did I say that?

I swallowed the lump in my throat and tried to cover my blunder. "So ... any questions?"

She shook her head. "Nope. Can I take these with me? Dad might see something that I missed."

"Of course." I carefully rolled up the plans and slid them into the tube.

"Wanna split the Tour of Italy?" she asked.

*More than anything.* I nodded, but inside I nearly cried.

No matter how much I tried to fight my feelings—she hadn't given any indication that she still had them for me—it was no use.

I'd fallen for Becky again.

Except for ceremoniously dropping the tomatoes from her salad into mine, she gave no indication she was even remotely interested in rekindling what we once had.

And try as I might, I couldn't bring myself to remember to call her Beck. It seemed so ... impersonal?

Our friendship—or whatever this was—was anything but.

# CHAPTER 8
## *Beck*

O h, *why* did I suggest the Tour of Italy? The expression on Willy's face—just for a second—was one of hope and affection. The very things I was feeling on the inside.

The very things I didn't want *him* to feel.

Feelings would complicate this job and undo all the years I spent trying to forget about him. Willy was and always would be the great love of my life. *Was* being the key word.

*Liam,* I chastised myself. *He's Liam now. Call him Liam! It's less personal. You cannot get personal!*

It was too late, though. I knew it. He probably knew it. There wasn't any way this *wouldn't* be personal, and no doubt Brenna knew it, too.

Brenna, under the guise of "hiring only the best" for her dream job, was no doubt taking full advantage of her match-making tendencies. In high school, she'd orchestrated the coupling of her best friend Chelsea to Liam's cousin, Jackson. And now that Kami, her college roommate, was single, Brenna was moving full speed ahead to get her and Trask together.

I had to admire her. As a natural matchmaker, she was born for wedding planning.

But Liam and I? Old news. I loved him too much to make him carry any more of my baggage. I was breaking under its weight, and it would be wrong to shift the load to him.

"So, Christmas ..." He let the word drag out.

My chin snapped up as his voice pulled me from my thoughts.

"Hmm?"

"Do you and your dad have plans? Will you be visiting your mom?"

I took a minute to gather my thoughts, toying with the napkin in my lap. "Mountainview has a dinner for residents and their families at noon."

He nodded. "So ... are you free Christmas night?"

My heart thundered in my chest. I wanted to scream *No!* but I couldn't get any sound out.

He cleared his throat. "Gran, uh, wanted me to invite you and your parents to her annual dessert party. I wasn't sure if your mom was able to leave Mountainview?"

"Oh, um ..." I scrambled for words. "No. She needs round-the-clock care, for basic needs. We're hoping she'll regain use of her legs after the experimental surgery. She'll still be wheel-chair-bound for quite some time, but having the use of her legs will give her more, um, personal mobility and freedom."

I didn't want to get into details. Mom had zero control over her bodily functions and wouldn't leave even if we asked her to.

The disappointment on his face tugged at my heart. "But ... Maybe Dad and I could stop by?"

His face brightened. "I'd—*Gran*—would like that."

I smiled. "Good. I've missed her a lot over the years." Thinking about Christmas made me think about celebrating all month long with his family. We'd spent many nights wandering the town park, all lit up, and attended all of Palmer City's events. "Does your family still attend the Christmas Eve Countdown to Christmas Carnival?"

He smiled. "We do. And Brodie has a booth this year."

My mouth gaped. "Little Brodie? What kind of booth?"

Liam's grin widened. "Not so little. He's the tallest in the family now and training to be a chocolatier. Gran made arrangements for him to use the bakery space after they close up in the days leading up to the event."

"No way." I was impressed. The scrappy Brodie, youngest of all the Brewer cousins, had always been small and stocky. The chocolate part didn't surprise me; the kid had consumed it like it was a food group.

"Way."

Our eyes connected, and I quickly averted my gaze. Our food arrived, and I kept the conversation focused on Liam's family, asking direct questions out of both curiosity and self-preservation. I didn't want to talk about me.

Not for a moment. Not at all.

This was already feeling like more than a business meeting. When the check arrived, Liam reached for it, but I insisted on splitting the bill. That's what business professionals would do, right?

I almost suggested going to Brewski's afterward, to lighten up the heavy tension that hadn't seemed to lift since I sat down, but decided against it. Brenna was working tonight, and the last thing I needed was to see her dart glances between us and beam like the Bat signal.

"Can I walk you to your car?" Liam asked as we stepped out into the cold night.

I shook my head. "I walked. It's not far."

He stopped and reached for my hand, then quickly let go. "Sorry. I—"

"It's okay," I replied. My throat betrayed me, drying out and forming a lump.

"I could walk you home, then?"

My eyes met his, and I nodded, unable to say no. But I took a step back, making sure there was plenty of space between us. "Sure. It's this way."

I turned on my boot heel, and he fell into step beside me. Ten minutes later, we arrived at the cottage Dad and I were renting. I stopped at the steps to the front porch and turned to him, unsure about what to say. We stood there, facing each other, hands in our pockets, and grappled for the right kind of goodbye that didn't seem too cool or too warm.

While I was struggling, he beat me to it.

"It was great spending time with you tonight," he said, pressing his lips together tightly as if to ensure he didn't say too much.

I could relate. My own lips were practically inside my mouth to keep my voice from betraying my brain. It would be so easy right now, in the soft glow of the moonlight, to spill all my thoughts and feelings to this man who had once known me better than I knew myself.

And probably still did.

His eyes shone with concern and unasked questions, and I couldn't look away.

I had to say something before he did. Before he asked something I didn't want to answer.

I broke eye contact and reached for my purse, rummaging around for my keys, and spoke hastily as guilt pounded through my veins. "So I'll see you at the barn tomorrow?" I asked him, still avoiding eye contact as my fingers closed around the keys.

"I'll be there."

*That voice.* The thick emotion behind the goosebump-inducing tenor made me want to confess every feeling ever.

I had to get inside. Quickly.

"Till tomorrow, then." I dared to look up at him.

"Goodnight, Becky."

I smiled. I loved how he said *Becky.* With a soft "kuh" unlike anyone else. I was glad I'd told him to call me that.

"Goodnight, Willy." I turned and fled into the house. Once inside, I snuck around to the front window and peeked out the side of the blinds to watch him leave.

Only he was still standing there, staring at the window I hid behind, as if he could see me and everything in my soul.

There was no way I was getting any sleep tonight.

# CHAPTER 9

## *Liam*

T hey say time flies when you're having fun.

I found a reason to be at the barn every day, and not just for structural purposes. With just Becky and her dad doing all the heavy labor, I couldn't see how we'd be able to stick to the timeline Brenna proposed.

Brendan was there almost as often as I was. It was obvious he held a torch for Brenna, and when I commented on it, the floodgates opened. I'd known that he knew Kingston, but it was news to me that he had looked up to him as a big brother and that Brenna had visited them once during a spring break when she was in college.

"I fell hook, line, and sinker," he told me, his gaze flicking across the barn to where she was conversing with Beck. "And I know she felt something for me—even now, I know it. But she's stubborn. Says she's too old for me. But I think there's something else holding her back. I'm not sure what that is, though."

"I know the feeling," I replied. I, too, knew what I wanted, but what did *Becky* want?

He sighed. "Ever been ice fishing?"

I shook my head.

"It's hours and hours of solitude, hoping and waiting to get a bite. But when you do, it's worth the wait. It teaches you patience and not to give up." He turned back to me, his eyes bright with determination and hope. "She's it for me. And I'm a very patient guy. I once went ice fishing for a week before I caught anything."

"Sounds miserable." I clapped him on the shoulder. "I see the way she steals looks at you when she doesn't think you're paying attention. She'll come around."

He nodded and tipped his chin. "And Beck? What's your story?"

I filled him in, and then we shared stories about Kingston. It was good to have someone to talk to who knew my family. I didn't have many friends in Rhode Island, and I knew that was on me. Every chance I had, every vacation I could get away, I'd come here to Palmer City instead of staying home or traveling with schoolmates or teammates or co-workers.

"Quitting time!" Brenna's announcement echoed through the chilly barn.

I checked my watch. It wasn't even four o'clock yet.

As if reading my mind, she continued. "Brendan, you have a flight to catch, or your mom will have my head. Beck, Estéban, Liam—I know you still have shopping to do. Christmas is in two days!"

We tidied up, said goodbye, and Brenna locked the barn. Since I needed to pick up Brodie at the bakery at five o'clock, I sat in my car for a bit instead of going back to the inn.

I only had another week to figure out what I was going to

do. If I was going to convince Becky we were better together, Christmas was an ideal time to try.

> Are you going to Countdown to Christmas?

I texted her.
Her reply arrived a few minutes later.

> You bet! See you there?

> You bet.

I grinned. Nostalgia would be on my side.

I shifted my car into gear and drove to the Sunflower Bakery to pick up my brother. The owner, Mrs. Hooper, was Gran's friend and had invited Brodie to use her commercial kitchen to make complicated chocolates and other confections for the carnival and our family's Christmas dessert party.

I parked out front and knocked on the glass door that sported a "CLOSED" sign. A pretty redhead with a long mass of curls stalked out the kitchen with a frown and a murderous glare in her eyes. I took a step back as she fiddled with the lock and opened the door.

"Well, get in with ya," she ordered in a thick Irish accent, holding the door open so I could squeeze by her. "Assuming yer Liam, that bloody arse Brodie's older brother. Maybe you can talk some sense into him. It's *my* kitchen when Miz Darlene isn't here, despite how long he's known her!" As her words sped up, they ran together and her consonants dropped.

I pressed my lips firmly together as I stepped inside to keep from laughing. She was clearly distressed, and that wasn't funny, but I knew my brother. He was a sucker for redheads and accents and for teasing girls he liked. I had a feeling we'd be seeing more of this one.

When I was sure I wouldn't laugh, I introduced myself, noticing Brodie slip out of the kitchen and head toward us. "I'm Liam. And you are?"

"Fyvie Kilchurn. Regretting that year abroad about now. The frigid coast of Belfast never looked so good. Your brother is the most *infuriating*—"

"Aw, Fy, you compliment me," Brodie called easily. "I've been called much worse."

She whirled on him. "And you'll be called worse if you don't get out of here in the next five minutes! Don't push me, Brewer."

He winked at her, which caused her to curse under her breath. "See you at the dessert party, then?"

"I'd rather break my back digging cockle shells on a frozen beach!" She narrowed her eyes at him and stalked back into the kitchen.

I grinned at him. "Always the charmer. What'd you do to her?"

He shrugged, but his eyes were twinkling. "Only told her that her methods were outdated and mine were better."

I shook my head. "You think she'll come to the party?"

"Oh yeah. I bet her my treats would go faster."

I snorted. "Of course you did."

"Couldn't help it. Help me carry them all out?"

We loaded over two dozen boxes of his gourmet chocolates and bite-size confections into the car, and I drove to Gran's, where he and my parents and our middle brother, Lawson, were staying.

"Mind if I take some for Beck?" I asked as we loaded them

into the extra fridge in the garage.

"Go for it. It'll give me a head start on my wager with Fyvie."

"What exactly am I helping you win?" I asked.

"Bragging rights. A summer job. And maybe the recipe for her chocolate. It's the best I've ever tasted."

"Ah. And I take it the lady doesn't want you around for that?"

He grinned. "So she says. But she goes back to Ireland at the end of June, so it's only a month she'd have to put up with me. Mrs. Hooper said I was welcome to work for myself or the bakery whenever I was in town. And I plan to be here whenever J&W isn't in session."

Brodie had been in elementary school when we moved to Rhode Island, and the change had been hard on him. He'd been Gran's little sidekick, always helping her in the kitchen and visiting Darlene Hooper at the bakery, "helping" them both since he could hold a wooden spoon. Both of them, along with Uncle Quinn, had been thrilled when he was accepted to Johnson & Wales and hoped he'd return to Palmer City someday.

I carefully filled a box for Beck and slid it into a gift bag I found in Gran's pantry before I added it to the fridge with the others.

*Knock, knock, knock.* "Mr. Liam!"

I opened the door to my suite the next morning to find little Hanna grinning up at me, hands behind her back. Her coat was unbuttoned, revealing a fuzzy Ninja Turtle onesie featuring Michelangelo's orange accents.

A girl after my own heart.

"Good morning," I said, leaning casually against the door frame.

"Cowabunga Merry Chrithsmas!" she squealed, shoving a card-size envelope at me. "Gramma said you weren't coming to breakfast, so Caitlyn said I had to d'liver your Chrithsmas card person-lee."

"She did, huh?" I took the envelope, and she ran away, giggling. As a precaution, I stepped outside.

Holding the envelope at arm's length, I jogged down the steps to the grass. I slid my finger under the flap and tore it open. Ever so slowly, I pulled the card out and opened it.

*Hwhoooosh!*

I coughed and jumped back, waving at the air as copious amounts of glitter floated to the ground. Giggling from behind the low hedge confirmed I was being watched. "Merry Christmas, girls!" I called. Laughing, I shook the card out onto the lawn and bent over to finger-comb the glitter out of my hair.

After a shower, I drove over to the farmhouse. Christmas Eve was an easy day for us Brewers, just hanging out and helping Gran and Gramps prep the farmhouse for Christmas Day. Mom, Aunt Patricia, Brenna, and Brodie helped Gran in the kitchen. Dad, Uncle Quinn, Aunt Angie, Keegan, and Drew were at Brewski's but would close up early so we could all walk to the park together. Kingston, Taylor, and Lawson were due to arrive this morning. Uncle Callum, Kingston and Jackson's dad, would pick them up at the airport. In the new barn, Gramps, Jackson, and I checked on the animals.

Swiftie was in a mood, snubbing me when I offered her

sugar cubes. I wondered if she missed Becky. I know I did.

After what felt like the longest Christmas Eve day ever, it was time to leave for Countdown to Christmas. We bundled up for the walk across the ranch to town. Behind us, the lights on Keegan's caboose blinked and danced for an audience of no one.

All that work. It was a shame the only people that would see it were family and the dessert party guests—if they trekked outside—since it was set so far back on the property.

My phone buzzed in the pocket of my long wool coat. Hoping it was Becky, I anxiously pulled it out and removed a glove so I could swipe to reply.

It *was* her. And she was already here.

> I see you! Dad and I are right behind you Brewers. 😊

I turned on my heel, and there she was, holding a steaming to-go cup in each hand, a shy smile on her face.

"Hot chocolate?" she offered, squinting at me. "Is that glitter in your eyebrow? Have you been crafting without me, Brewer?"

I took a cup from her and snuck in a side hug. "Thanks. The Warner girls' Christmas card featured a glitter bomb."

She snorted and reached up to brush it away in a tender gesture that made me want more contact. I craved her touch, even something so small and innocent like this.

I said hello to her father and introduced him to the family members he hadn't met yet. He and my dad fell fast into easy conversation about some construction project on the road to Elk Creek Falls.

Becky lifted on her toes and whispered in my ear. "I think

they like each other."

I laughed. It sure did look that way.

We made our way through the brightly lit park to the stage that was set up in front of the towering Christmas tree and gathered in a group behind the rows of already-full wooden benches. Countdown to Christmas was part festival, with vendors lining the perimeter, and part stage show. Ten booths featured Christmas cookies, including Brodie's, where his no-bake crisped rice and marshmallow wreaths garnished with red M&Ms were disappearing quickly. There would be ten acts on the stage, ending with Mrs. Claus inviting kids to sit with her while she read "'Twas the Night Before Christmas." Each child brought a gift-wrapped book to exchange later, colored-coded by age recommendation. It was a tradition I'd loved as a kid.

Somehow, the committee had landed the internationally famous sibling singing group The Harbor Lights. Dean, Chase, and Macy Wells had just released a Christmas album and were spending the week with their family in Colorado Springs.

I closed my eyes as their soothing vocal arrangement of "Silent Night" washed a wave of peace over me. Becky's arm pressed against mine, and I wondered if she was also thinking of a conversation we'd had long ago, of how silent nights were the best nights in her household.

Next up was ... Keegan? The curtains parted, revealing one of those string-light trees he had on his lawn, plus three cartoonish light-bulb cutouts with LED faces. A large, pixe-lated screen hung center stage. As the bulbs "sang" "*The Twelve Days of Christmas,*" images of the gifts named in the song danced on the screen and twirled on the tree.

By the joyful exclamations around us, he hadn't told

anyone in our family he'd applied to the event. It was a hard act to follow, but the resident club of cloggers, and high school chemistry teacher Mr. Brigden with his Christmas magic act, held the crowd's attention.

Becky and I were still shoulder-to-shoulder, and when I felt her shaking from the cold during the high school dance team's performance, I wrestled with keeping my arm to myself. But when she leaned her head on me, I went for it. I closed my eyes and snaked my arm around her, ecstatic when she leaned into me.

More acts followed before Mrs. Claus, and we didn't move or shift once through the Christmas Comedian (who was really the elementary school principal, whose jokes got cornier every year) or the community theater's Grinch skit.

Just the two of us, pseudo-snuggling at the town's Christmas Countdown, as we had many times in the past. I stared straight ahead, ignoring the side glances and smiles from my friends and relatives.

I shouldn't get my hopes up.

But they were already soaring as high as Santa's sleigh.

Mrs. Claus ended the story and closed her book, which was the cue for the kids to place their books on tables that had been set up at the back of the stage. Becky and I stayed to watch as they formed a line to choose their books and get a hug from Mrs. Claus. Parents collected their children as they stepped off the stage, and within minutes, the crowd had cleared, leaving only the stragglers without Santa-age children milling about.

I bent my arm and leaned over to whisper in Becky's ear. "Can I walk you home?"

She met my gaze and nodded. "Let me just tell my dad."

# CHAPTER 10

*Beck*

It was Christmas Day, and I was antsy. I *should not* be worried about the Brewers' dessert party. I should be fully present here at Mountainview, with my reconnected mom and dad, every kid's dream, enjoying the holiday.

More than once, Dad had to tap me on the shoulder to bring me out of my thoughts. Mom just kept smiling her little secret smile like she knew what I was thinking.

She probably did. Willy was always in my thoughts back then and certainly now.

"Do you think this dress is okay?" I blurted right into the middle of a sentence Dad was speaking.

They turned to me, and I immediately pressed my lips together. "Sorry!" Averting my gaze, I smoothed the full skirt of my cranberry A-line fifties-style dress with a fitted, button-up bodice and sheer puffed sleeves. I suddenly wondered if it was too much.

"Beck," Dad replied evenly, if not a little reproachfully. "You could be wearing Santa's sack and Liam wouldn't care. If that's what you're worried about."

"That's what I'm afraid of," I mumbled. "I don't want him getting any ... ideas."

*Why not?* Mom scrolled on her whiteboard. *You two are meant for each other.*

"Because ..." How could I phrase an answer that wouldn't hurt her feelings? Mom held a ton of guilt for the horribleness that was my childhood. I decided to go with another angle. "He lives across the country."

She waved a hand flippantly, as if the distance didn't matter, and returned her marker to the board. *Please. I bet you need only say the word and he'll be back here in a heartbeat. Permanently. That was always the plan, wasn't it?*

"It was, before—" I zipped my lips. "It's been a long time, that's all. We're different people now."

"As are your mother and I." Dad looked at Mom so sweetly I got an instant toothache. "Distance hasn't changed how we feel about each other, though." He cleared his throat and flashed her a boyish grin "If anything, it has made my heart grow fonder."

*And mine,* Mom wrote, her eyes glimmering with unshed tears.

I nearly cried, seeing my mother beam at his words. She'd spent the last two and a half *decades* experiencing heartache, abuse, and then living with a significant physical disability. My heartbreak over Liam must look like a shallow blip to her.

I breathed out a long sigh in an attempt to gather myself together. "Okay, well ... You sure you don't want to come with me?"

Mom shook her head, scrawling furiously on the board. *You go, and have a wonderful time. And if Quinn Brewer baked those peanut butter and almond cookies, maybe sneak me some?*

I laughed. "Of course." Willy's Uncle Quinn didn't just own Brewski's; he was an award-winning chef and baker. One Christmas, Brodie showed up at our door with a box of cookies he'd baked with his uncle and grandmother. Mom went nuts over the peanut butter and almond ones and has probably dreamed about them every night since the last time she had one.

I hugged them goodbye and gave myself a pep talk on the way to my car. Really, I shouldn't be nervous at all. The Brewers had welcomed me back into their fold like no time had passed, like I'd never left or ghosted anyone. I knew I didn't deserve their kindness, so the guilt was eating away at my confidence.

Willy's grandparents' farmhouse was lit up with strings of icicle lights. Soft white bulbs wound around the pine trees on either side of the house. I parked on the massive lawn a few cars down from Brenna's.

On the verge of chickening out, I texted him to let him know I'd arrived. As I unbuckled my seat belt, I caught a beam of light in my peripheral vision from the front door. I grinned, unable to see who it was with the light behind him but knowing without a doubt it was the recipient of my text.

I slid out of the car as he approached. In his hand, he held a white box. "For you. For later," he said, holding it up. "Brodie's best."

"Peanut butter and almond cookies?" I asked.

His face fell. "No, but I can get you some."

I took the box and peered through the clear window. "Oooh!" Inside was an assortment of fancy chocolates. "Yeah, I'm not sharing these. But I do need to steal some cookies for my mom."

"I can do that for you. I have connections, you know," he teased.

I opened the door and set the box on the seat. "Do you, now?"

"I do. How do you think I got these?"

I laughed, then lifted my chin to meet his eyes. "Thank you. I'm such a dunce. I didn't think to bring anything for the party—or you."

Actually, I *had* thought about getting him something, but then I chickened out. I was sure it would send mixed signals.

Couldn't have that.

Wasn't ready for that.

"All I—*we*—want is for you to be here." He took a step closer to me, and all that was between us were a few inches and the puffs of steam from our breath. It was cold, but in that moment, all I felt was warmth. "You belong, here, Becky."

My puffs of breath stopped as I processed his words. "I'm h-h-appy to be here," I stuttered.

I needed to get inside before this turned into more of a *moment* than it already was. I turned to the side and linked my arm into his like we'd done last night. "Let's go in."

We strolled across the lawn, and he held the door open for me. His grandpa was right inside and greeted me with a hug and an offer to take my coat and hat.

I was overwhelmed with embraces and consumed more sugar than one should, even at Christmas. After an hour or so, I was ready to leave.

But a part of me didn't want to. I'd always felt like I was a part of this family, and being back with them made me feel whole again.

Willy still knew me so well. He hadn't left my side, no doubt sensing that I needed his support.

Just like he could always sense when something was off.

"Wanna take a walk?" he whispered after an animated conversation with his brothers and cousins. Brodie and their middle brother, Lawson, were debating how far the Denver Edge would make it this season, much to the annoyance of Kingston, whose team was ahead of the Edge in the points standings.

"Yes, let's."

I loved watching hockey and understood the rules and nuances of the game well, but I was lost when it came to stat talk and trade deadlines and waivers and operations lingo.

We retrieved our coats and slipped out the kitchen door. I linked my arm through his again and let him lead, though I knew his intended destination.

The new barn housed the family's horses, and my heart skipped a beat in anticipation of seeing Swiftie. He'd been the best kind of therapy for me until I moved away.

More than just an escape from the verbal abuse and constant dressing-downs, the Brewer family ranch was a happy playground and safe place to dream.

Willy punched in the code, and one of the doors slid open. This was way fancier than the old barn. I wondered why Brenna hadn't asked for automatic doors? Perhaps they weren't rustic enough for her wedding venue vision?

"Hey, boy." We stopped at the first stall, and Willy opened the gate. Swiftie neighed and whinnied in delight. "Don't get too excited. I didn't bring you any Christmas treats. I know Gran was here spoiling you earlier."

The horse snorted and shuffled his front legs in response.

I laughed and reached a hand out to stroke his cheek. "Merry Christmas, Swiftie." His nose twitched, and then he was nuzzling my neck. I glanced at Willy, who had a faraway look in his eyes. We had so many good times with this horse, from that first summer taking turns bottle-feeding him to teaching him how to move with riders, to hitching him up to the wagon with all the younger kids riding in the back.

I reached around his neck to hug him close. My eyes shut, and more memories sprang forth in a flood. Feeling a strong hand rubbing my back sympathetically, I remembered how important those times were.

"I missed you, too, Swiftie. More than you could ever know." I opened my eyes and locked them on Willy's. He had to know I was referring to him, too.

Suddenly, Swiftie neighed and shuffled back and with a little push of his head, knocked me off balance. I stumbled into Willy, whose arms fanned out as he went down.

I landed on top of him with a *thump*. Swiftie's whinnies sounded like laughter, and I wondered if he'd done it on purpose.

Willy grinned and made no move to get up or push me aside. Instead, he reached up to straighten my cloche hat, his hand lingering on the brim before it trailed to my face and along my jaw. The tenderness and sincerity in his eyes would have knocked me off my feet if I hadn't already been lying on the ground.

I also made no attempt to move. *Stupid! What are you thinking? Get up!*

But my body wasn't listening to my brain. "I think he did that on purpose," I whispered. "Silly horse." Willy was so close. On impulse, I straightened his glasses and then my fingers took on a mind of their own. Mimicking his move, I traced the line of his short beard along his jawline.

"Smart horse," he said. "Good horse. Becky, I ..."

I didn't know what he was going to say, and I wasn't sure I was ready to hear it. So I silenced him.

With a kiss.

*Now you've done it!*

But I didn't care. I needed this. I needed to know how he felt about me. If he still felt the way we used to.

From the way he kissed me back, I was pretty sure he felt *something*.

*Good horse, indeed.*

# Shining Star Barn Events

*Brenna's To-Do List*

**Who:** Ranford-Brewer Wedding Squared
**When:** June

### 7 Months Before—*November*

√ *Clear out barn*

√ *Reunite Liam and Beck so they realize their HEA is with each other*

### 6 Months Before—*December*

√ *Contact electrician and plumber*

√ *Finalize task lists with Beck and schedule all subcontractors*

### 5 Months Before—*January*

___ *Order tables and chairs*

___ *Meet with Taylor and Chelsea to finalize accent colors for reception*

### 4 Months Before—*February*

___ *Schedule cake tasting and all the catering things. CAKE IS FOR BRIDE AND GROOM. DO NOT EAT THE CAKE, NO MATTER HOW MANY TIMES MRS. HOOPER OFFERS. BE STRONG!*

___ *Finalize everything floral*

### 3 Months Before—*March*

___ *Order linens and dishware*

___ *Hire an assistant*

Notes:

~~*Liam can't travel until Thanksgiving.~~

~~*Beck's business license is still waiting on approval.~~

~~Vibe: Neither seem to feel the urgency (to get together). C'mon, people!~~

*Talk to Aunt Patricia about using her box at the arena for a "family" Valentine's Day outing. Get Liam and Beck to attend <u>BY ANY MEANS NECESSARY</u>. Maybe for a "progress check?"

*Is there time to construct a gazebo?

# CHAPTER 11

## *Liam*

Returning home to my empty, cold apartment in Rhode Island reminded me of everything I'd left behind. All I could think about was that epic kiss in the barn and the smaller, sweeter, stolen kisses over the next week.

But when I'd bent for a goodbye kiss on my way to the airport, Becky placed a finger over my lips and hugged me instead, so tightly I gasped for air. Then she backed away and ran to her car without another word. I knew she was struggling with what to make of our reconnection, and I hoped this time apart would help her realize how much we belonged together.

After a particularly frustrating workday at the end of January, I sat back in my recliner to text her. Lawson had just been hired at a major airline. With the job came family perks, which had me thinking about my next trip to Colorado. Whenever it was, it couldn't come soon enough.

Before I could draft a message to Becky, a text from Brenna scrolled across my screen.

Hey cuz! You have V-day plans?

I snorted.

You know I don't. Why?

'Cause we're all going to the Volts game.
Beck, too. Can you get away?

My nerves began to tingle, and my heart rate kicked up.
My cousin was brilliant.

I'd never tell her that, though.

A group outing would be minimal pressure and still give
me an opportunity to ask Becky to be my Valentine.

Was it too early to cash in that offer from my brother?
Nah.

I can,

I replied.

You'll get me a ticket?

You bet! And Liam?

Yeah?

Make a move, already. Beyond all the shy
smooching when you thought no one was
watching. TELL HER HOW YOU FEEL.

I frowned.

You saw us?

Everybody did.

I didn't know how to feel about that.

Is she upset about it?

She hasn't said anything so if you're clueless, she probably is, too.

Okay phew.

Dude, seriously? I repeat: TELL HER HOW YOU FEEL.

You really think that's a good idea?

Yup. She talks about you A LOT. Every day.

Yes! I closed my eyes and pumped my fist in the air.

She's all I think about, Bren.

I know. So do something about it!

Yes, ma'am!

I couldn't text Becky fast enough.

Roses are red,

The Volts wear blue,

Whaddaya think

of me spending V-day with you?

KEEP ME IN MIND

I snorted. That was *really* bad.

I didn't have to wait long for her response.

> Bring me some chocolate
>
> In a little red box
>
> And I'll say yes
>
> And enjoy it a lots.

I laughed. Okay, hers was worse. I leaned forward as more bad rhymes filled my head.

> I'll raid Brodie's stash
>
> And choose the best bits
>
> I'll do anything you ask
>
> If you'll grant me a kiss.

I waited.

And waited. My stomach growled, reminding me I hadn't eaten dinner. Why was she taking so long to reply? Being my Valentine was okay but not a kiss? Was she having second thoughts?

An hour later, I nearly jumped from the couch when my phone vibrated in my pocket.

> We'll see about that
>
> The old blurs with the new
>
> How can I be sure
>
> How I feel about you?

My shoulders slumped. I was one hundred percent sure of how I felt about her.

Always had been.

I refused to believe she didn't know that. I was sure her fears were anchored in separating again if we got back together. Assuring her I was in this forever was what I needed to do.

> If you feel as I do
>
> Then there's no debate
>
> Forever is waiting
>
> I've no doubt it's our fate.

Brenna said to tell her how I felt. This ought to do that. I took a deep breath and hit "send."

I was falling asleep to the Denver versus Boston hockey game when Becky's next reply came through.

> My heart is yours
>
> If you'll claim it for keeps.
>
> But distance is against us
>
> And it makes me weep.

Before I could reply, another quatrain from her appeared.

> If you want forever
>
> I must be assured
>
> That my heart is safe

> And properly secured.

Oh, I would properly secure her heart all right. No doubt about that.

> You know I will.
>
> I always have.
>
> Let me prove to you
>
> My love is a salve.

Maybe not the best choice of words, but it got my point across.

> Let's take it slow, then
>
> Start easy and small.
>
> Then build if it's to be,
>
> And knock down the walls.

I wanted to type back that I'd gather up whatever tools it would take to tear down her walls. But I had a feeling this was already a lot for one night.

I'd focus on getting myself prepared to go all in on Valentine's Day. What was something that wouldn't leave any doubt in her mind? Something that proved I was one hundred percent committed to her, like I had when we were teenagers? That I meant every word and that I wanted to move back to Colorado to prove it.

*Like I had when we were teenagers* ... That was it!

*The promise ring!* I slid my hand into my pocket and rolled it between my fingers. But how did you give something back to someone who'd literally buried it in the past? Was I setting myself for heartbreak all over again?

CHAPTER 12

*Beck*

Exchanging short poems with Willy last night had me both hopeful and on edge the next morning. I stayed in bed longer than usual and waited until Dad left for the barn before getting ready. Afraid that he'd be able to see something was up by reading my face, I texted him that my head hurt (which it did, though figuratively) and I'd be along later. I needed time to get myself together.

And coffee. A big, strong, Bevvie Bar cup of coffee.

I never made it to the barn. Before I could get into my car, Dad texted that Mom had been approved for the surgery. Since this phase of the project was all us—no subcontractors—he would close up the barn for the day to go tell her. He wanted to be there whenever the doctor showed up to learn more about the process and how to support her.

I decided he probably needed coffee, too. At the Bevvie Bar, I stepped into line behind Brendan and Xavier and waved hello. They'd been a big help over the last few months, moving heavy things and volunteering for odd jobs.

"Beck!" Brendan pulled me in for a hug. "Can you believe

this guy? Swanny here has never been to the Bevvie Bar? I mean, do you even live in Palmer City if you've never been here?"

I laughed. Brendan had been here all of seven months.

Xavier shrugged. "I don't drink coffee, man. It tastes foul."

Brendan rolled his eyes. "Please do not insult the magical liquid, especially in front of the barista. Penny might banish us both."

A snort from behind them caused them to whirl around. Penny Palmer was the sweetest girl you ever met. Shy with long, honey-brown hair, she wouldn't have banished a fly.

"I dare you to order a coffee," Brendan challenged.

"I'm good," Xavier insisted.

"I triple dog dare you to order a coffee."

Now I was laughing.

But Xavier wasn't. I could only see half his face, but he looked horrified.

"It's not *that* bad," I assured him. "Unless you're allergic?"

He shook his head. "No. But he *triple dog dared* me."

I looked at Brendan to explain.

He smirked triumphantly. "Hockey players are superstitious. Everyone on our team this year who's ignored a triple dog dare has played a horrible game afterward."

"Ah," I said. "Well, maybe Penny can make it taste like something else."

Xavier's gaze landed on the doughnut display, then he looked to Penny, not speaking for a moment. Her cheeks pinked, but she didn't say a word, either. Penny had a terrible stutter and only spoke when she absolutely had to. In the corner of the café, her harp stood sentry, waiting for her expert fingers to stroke the cords during slow times. She played beautifully, and I often came just to listen when I felt overwhelmed.

"Can you make it taste like that toffee crunch doughnut?" he asked, almost whispering.

She nodded and smiled and, a few moments later, placed a lid on a concoction topped with whipped cream, dusted with toffee bits, and drizzled with caramel. Grinning widely, she scooted down the counter to set it in the pickup tray.

It almost made me decide to change my order.

Penny set about making Brendan's drink next, and we continued to chat until the soft chime on the door signaled a new arrival.

"Beck!" I turned to find Brenna hurrying toward me. "I was just at the barn and ran into your dad locking up. Such amazing news!" She reached out and clutched my forearms. "What can I do?"

I inhaled deeply, unsure how to respond. What could she do? And why?

*Why,* because she was Brenna Brewer. And despite years and years of no contact, she was still my friend. Even though I'd been a terrible friend to her. I didn't deserve the help—or the grace—she was offering.

"What can I get you?" Tasha, Penny's sister and also a barista, asked. "Oh, hey Beck. Brenna. The usuals?"

"Thanks, Tasha," Brenna said, nodding. "And whatever her dad orders. I'm buying."

"No, no," I protested, rummaging in my purse. But she was faster and tapped her card on the pin pad before I could get mine out. "Really, Brenna, there's nothing to do."

"Then we celebrate."

"What are we celebrating?" Brendan asked from down the counter.

Brenna's cheeks reddened. "Phase one, surgery approval. Her mother's spine surgery, you dunce."

"Hold up," I pleaded. "Isn't it too early to celebrate? What if it doesn't work? We'll jinx it." I wasn't superstitious, but it felt wrong celebrating the success of something that hadn't happened yet.

"You don't believe that," she disagreed softly as we scooted down the counter to wait for our drinks.

Brendan placed his palms together. "We're all praying for her, Beck. She's going to do great."

"Thanks." I was praying for it, too.

Brenna handed me two of the to-go cups. "Now get over there, learn all the things, and call me later, okay?"

I nodded, slightly dazed. "Okay."

Dad was pacing in a corner of the empty lobby on his phone when I arrived at Mountainview Manor. He held up a finger, signaling me to wait.

"Uh-huh. Sí. Yes ... Understood. Thank you." He tapped his screen and strode over to me in three long steps, took the drinks from my hand and placed them on the reception desk. He enveloped me in a stifling hug, murmuring words in Spanish I couldn't understand.

Tears stung in my eyes. I guessed I hadn't fully processed the gravity of what was happening until that moment. "It's okay, Dad. It's okay."

"It's not okay, but I will make amends, amorcito. Make everything right. I never should have left. I should have trusted my gut and my heart, no matter how hard or impossible the path ahead with your mother seemed. Her parents hated me, and they were threatening to throw her out. I thought she'd be better off without me. I never told you this ... I joined the army to keep myself far away, to try to forget her. But I never did. How could I? *Every day* I thought of her, missed her, wondered what she was doing, where she was, if she'd found someone else, if she was happy. And I could never have imagined how wrong my choice to leave her would be. All those years we wasted apart ... all the pain she suffered, physically, emotionally, mentally ... I missed your first seventeen years. It was all so agonizing and so unnecessary."

I listened, my heart cracking at the anguish behind his words. Many times, I'd wondered how different our lives would have been if he'd stayed. I'd never have moved in next door to Willy, of that I was sure.

But he *had* left. And that was in the past. It was too painful to keep playing "What if?"

I had to reassure him. "You're here now, Dad. The past is just that—the past." I squeezed him tight. "You're here now," I repeated firmly.

"Yes. I am here. Never leaving again. I promise." He sighed. "Your advice is good, amor. Wise. Like it's from someone who knows how I feel." He stepped back and held me at arm's length. "I have so many regrets. My pride cost me many years of happiness. I was heartbroken, alone, empty, living life in robot mode. I learned construction to keep my hands and mind busy and distracted."

"Oh, Dad," I cried, flinging my arms around his middle. I'd done the same thing. "I don't know what to do."

"What is your heart telling you?" His voice was soft, his tone soothing and gentle. "I know what my eyes are telling me. You are in love with him. When you look at him, it is how your mother looked upon me, long ago. Liam is in love with you. He always has been. I watch him. He is attentive, affectionate, kind in ways that come naturally to a man in love. Don't be afraid to give him your heart. He won't hurt it, of that I am sure."

"How can you be so certain? You hardly know him," I mumbled into his flannel shirt.

He kissed the top of my head and stepped back again. Our teary gazes locked. "I just *know*. Faith. Fate. Regardless, the barn project is a gift that brought you two back together, much like your mother's accident was for her and I. That may have been the worst day of your life, but it was the best day of mine, because it set in motion the events that brought me back to her. And to you. The day I was called into my superior's office and told I had a daughter and she was coming to Germany was the answer to many prayers."

The realization hit me like a lightning bolt. Mom's fall, the tragedy that it was, had also been the catalyst for my parents' reconnection and reclaimed happiness. I nodded slowly, taking in his words and advice and mulling it over.

He was right.

"Amorcito, it's your life and your decision. But don't be afraid to live it."

My heart was heavy under the weight of his words. I swiped at my eyes to unblur the image of the man before me. A deep understanding passed between us, and I felt our connection strengthen. In this bittersweet moment, I felt a glimmer of hope for the future.

Not just Mom's future or hers with Dad.

My future, too.

With them, and with William Brewer.

Because a future without him would be what Dad had experienced all those years without Mom. I'd already had a taste of that emptiness and need for distraction, living in the robot mode he spoke about and compartmentalizing my heartache for a love long lost.

I couldn't rewrite the past. But Willy and I could build a future together. Our story didn't have to end on that fateful night nine and a half years ago.

Dad was right. I'd live with so many regrets if I didn't give us a fair shot. If I let fear keep me from the one person who knew everything about me and still wanted me by his side, all day, every day.

I had to find a way to heal the old wounds and move forward to embrace the love—and the man—that had never given up on me.

# CHAPTER 13

# *Liam*

"**R**ace you to the top, Willy!" Kingston let go of Auntie Patricia's hand and dropped his lunchbox on the grass.

I raced after him toward the playground, anxious to prove I was quicker and assert myself as the fastest Brewer on the first day of kindergarten.

"Oh no you don't!" Brenna's chirpy threat came from behind me, but she soon passed both of us and was the first to reach the base of the rock-climbing wall.

We'd climbed this wall many times. It was a larger version of the one at my grandparents' house. We were all pretty evenly matched. Kingston was small but fast. I was taller with longer legs and could skip some of the climbing holds. Brenna was strategic, always finding the fastest route to the top.

I pulled ahead of Brenna, and then Kingston, and barely beat them both over the top. "King of the wall!" I shouted.

"Today," Kingston retorted, giving me a light shove. "You know I'll beat you tomorrow."

"You boys are so dumb." Brenna thumbed her finger over her shoulder. "I'm going to go make a new friend. Bye!"

*Behind her, sitting in the corner of the platform in a pink dress and dark brown pigtails, was the frowny little girl who'd moved in next door to me a few days ago. She hugged her knees to her chest. It made me sad to see her sad.*

*"Race you down the tire wall, across the monkey bars, and back to our moms?" Kingston proposed.*

*"Uh …" I glanced at the new girl again, wide-eyed but curious as Brenna jabbered about girly stuff. She was so pretty.*

*"Willy! On your mark … get set … go!"*

*It took me a second to register that he'd just challenged me, but then I was off. I had to beat him.*

*And I did, but just barely. Mom handed me my lunchbox, and I looked up to the platform. Brenna and the new girl were watching.*

*She was smiling.*

*And at five years old, I knew without a doubt that I was in love.*

"Please return your seats and tray tables to their upright position …"

I opened my eyes, reluctantly ending the daydream. Part of me longed for the simpler days of my youth, when I was still innocent and believed evil only lived in make-believe worlds, not in parental figures who lived next door. When we played pretend and slayed imaginary dragons because we couldn't win against the human one.

It was just after one o'clock when I arrived at my rental car. The brisk Colorado mountain air filled my lungs, a stark contrast to the heavy, salty mist I'd left behind in Providence.

My heart raced with anticipation and nervousness as I drove to the assisted living facility. On the seat next to me were the peanut butter and toasted almond cookies Becky's mother loved so much. I bribed Brodie with hockey tickets to make me a couple of batches of Uncle Quinn's recipe.

It had been almost a decade since I'd last seen Mrs. Monroe. Up until recently, I hadn't had any desire to see the woman who was responsible for Beck's miserable childhood. But I'd learned since then that life was complicated. My mother had offered another perspective, having seen and comprehended more with her adult eyes during that time than a child or young teen ever could have.

Essentially, Becky's mother felt trapped. For her, there was no way out. Unbeknownst to me, my parents had offered to help her countless times, and she'd always refused, insisting her husband was never violent, was a good provider, and she loved him. My mother hadn't believed her, but without evidence of abuse or a complaint from Becky or her mom, there wasn't anything that could be done.

The drive felt endless, and with each mile, the weight of the amends I had to make became heavier.

I signed in at the desk. The receptionist issued me a sticker nametag and asked me to wait while she verified that Becky's mother would see me.

She returned a few moments later and waved me to follow her down the cheerfully wall-papered hall to the last room on the left. There, Mrs. Monroe sat in a mauve recliner, fragile but beautiful as ever, her honey-blond hair falling in waves over her shoulder. Becky had her mother's face and stature and her father's dark hair and strength.

Gesturing to the empty facility-issued chair beside her, she invited me to sit. I knew she'd lost her voice in the accident, but her eyes spoke the volumes her lips couldn't vocalize.

I approached slowly and handed her the box of cookies. "Hi, Mrs. Monroe. I—I'm sorry it took me so long to come and see you. I brought you these."

Her eyes lit up with recognition and gratitude. She accepted the box and set it on the bed beside her, then reached for a whiteboard and marker.

*Thank you! These are my favorite. Please call me Cathy,* she wrote with trembling hands. *Mrs. Monroe is in the past.*

Tears welled up in my eyes as I read her words. Becky hadn't mentioned if she'd changed her name, and the receptionist had known who I was talking about. But I didn't want to ask.

Taking a deep breath, I replied, "I came to tell you how much I love your daughter. I always have. And I'm praying— my whole family is—for your surgery to be successful."

Her eyes glistened with unshed tears as she erased the message on the board to begin a new one. *I'm sorry for being a terrible mother when Becky was growing up. I wish I'd been strong enough to stand up to him.*

My heart ached as I read her confession, the weight of years of guilt and regret etched on her face. I reached out and gently took her hand, squeezing it reassuringly.

"You were always there for her in your own way," I whispered, my voice thick with emotion. "And you did the best you could. He never laid a finger on her. I'm sorry I judged you back then. I was a dumb kid."

She smiled, but her eyes were filled with sadness. She let go of my hand and turned back to the board, writing for several minutes before she turned it around for me to read.

*It wasn't nearly enough. I should have faced my parents and ran away with Estéban. And I never should have married Dirk. I was a terrible mother, allowing him to treat her as he did and perpetuating the lie that she was lacking because she was born early. He had impossible expectations. I didn't want her to feel bad, so I made that up. I did so many wrong things ... You and your family were more of a family to Becky than her own was. Thank you for being there for her then. And thank you for being there for her now.*

My heart ached as I read her confession and apology. I swallowed, knowing what I wanted to say and hoping it came out clearly. "I want to be there for her in the future, too," I confessed. "Will you give me your blessing?" I didn't need her permission to pursue Becky again, but it was important to me that she was supportive.

She patted my hand and smiled while she wrote. *You've always had it, you dear dear boy.*

I couldn't hold back my tears any longer, and they fell down my cheeks as I leaned in to hug her. She pulled me close, her shuddery silent sobs echoing the depth of her emotions.

As we held each other, the door creaked open, and Becky appeared on the other side of her mother's chair. I opened my eyes to see her wearing a mixture of surprise and concern on her face. I let go and returned to my seat as she pulled her mom to her in a protective embrace, holding her close and looking like she never wanted to let go.

"What are you doing here?" she whispered softly.

I didn't want to get into all the reasons. "I wanted to see your mom. Wish her well on her surgery and let her know my family and I were praying for her."

She nodded as her mother pulled away and picked up the whiteboard, wiping away her tears and writing hurriedly. *He brought me cookies. Have one. ONE. Ha ha.*

Becky chuckled, and it was enough to break the tension.

Her mother erased the words, and we leaned in to read her

next message. *I know you two have big plans tonight. Go to the hockey game and have fun.*

I looked at Becky, happy to see joy in her eyes. It was clear to me that my visit to see her mother meant a lot to her.

We left shortly after, leaving her mom to her thoughts and the cookies. I knew that, just like her mother's affection for those cookies, our affection for each other would always be a sweet and enduring bond. Unlike the cookies, I wouldn't let that bond crumble ever again.

As we walked down the corridor, hand in hand, I thought about families. I knew I'd been incredibly fortunate to grow up in a loving home with siblings I got along well with and part of a big extended family that gathered regularly. Growing up, my cousins had been my best friends.

I wanted to continue that legacy, invite Becky into my family officially and start our own tight home unit that would be like the one I grew up in.

# CHAPTER 14

## *Beck*

After the emotionally charged scene at Mountainview Manor it took me a while to adjust my countenance for the Voltage game. I drove home to drop off my car and then hopped in Willy's. We enjoyed a long early dinner at the inn. He snuck in Brodie's chocolates for dessert, and I wished he'd brought more. His brother had a true talent for creating the confections—even if his chocolate wasn't as good as Fyvie's.

I'd never say that out loud, though.

At the arena, the Brewers were as warm and welcoming as ever. Willy's Aunt Patricia and cousin Jackson's medical group was affiliated with the team, so they had a corporate viewing box with a small event room and a section of cushy seats that offered a great view.

The arena was alive with excitement. The crowd pulsed with energy. The players, adorned in pink and red jerseys sprinkled with hearts, presented a fitting tribute to the sentiment of the holiday.

The star center from the opposing team skated over to the penalty box, which meant the Volts were on the power play.

"Charge up, Volts!" I shouted. Willy and his brothers and cousins had all played hockey growing up, so I had a basic understanding of the game.

Five of the Volts' best players skated to the ice to go up against four members of the opposing team, whose task would be to kill the penalty minutes. The centers bent into position for the puck drop, and our team got possession when Maddox Knott's stick was first to the puck.

"YEAH!" Only three minutes were left in the game, and we were up a man for two of them. The excitement was as high as it could go. If our guys scored, we'd tie the game and likely go to overtime.

"Oooh! Find the hole!" Brenna yelled. I giggled. She'd played goalie up through middle school. She elbowed me. Hard. "Look at their netminder's position! That's sloppy. He's only got one defender on their penalty kill. No way should he leave the crease exposed like that."

No sooner had she uttered her last word than one of the Volts did just that. Xavier Schwann, from the red line in the center of the ice, sent the puck sailing through traffic and straight over the goalie's right shoulder to the back of the net. His teammates jumped on him in celebration as the lamp over the goal lit up.

"Yeah, Swanny! Yeah!" I screamed.

"Tied!" Brenna's younger brother, Drew, confirmed the obvious, and I giggled again.

I hadn't had this much fun since ... Gosh, I couldn't remember when. It was like old times, before Willy moved and my world came crashing down. Literally.

But this game was not destined to go into overtime. The Voltage dominated the ice and didn't allow the other team to gain possession. With ten seconds left on the clock, right winger Rurik Antonov, behind the opposing net, caught a pass from Brendan and slid it around the pipe and over the blue paint of the crease before the goalie could block it.

The horn blared, signaling the end of the game, and we cheered like they'd just won a championship. Plans were made to go to Brewski's. The team celebrated their wins there, in the function room.

"Are you coming to Brewski's?" Willy asked. "Or do you want to do something else?" His stare penetrated my soul, almost as if the question held more than surface-level significance.

I was glad he didn't ask if I wanted to go home. "I'd like to go to Brewski's. It's been forever since I've been to an after-party. Do the players still come out of the function room and chat with the fans?"

"Most do," he replied. He dropped his chin, his mouth curving up into a boyish smile as his glasses slid down his nose.

I gently pushed them back up the bridge with my forefinger. "Cool." But I didn't really care anymore about meeting the athletes. I just wanted to be by Willy's side, sharing shepherd's pie bites and lemonade and listening to him and his cousins recount the best and the worst plays of the game.

The party at Brewski's was everything I remembered and imagined it would be. The restaurant buzzed with laughter and excitement as the team joined us to celebrate their victory. I watched Willy's face light up, surrounded by athletes, friends, and his family. It was a joyous occasion, and I couldn't help but be swept up in the happiness of it all.

As the night wore on, I leaned over and whispered in his

ear, "I'm having a great time. Thank you for making this Valentine's Day so special."

He turned to me, his eyes filled with warmth and affection. "I'm just glad you're here with me."

But I could tell there was something more he wanted to say, something on his heart. He took my hand and led me outside. We walked together in the crisp night air until we reached the barn, a place that held so many memories for us, then and now.

Willy spun the dial on the padlock. Once inside, I flicked on the lights. The barn looked nothing like its old self. It had disappeared into the past, with the younger versions of us.

He pulled me to him, his expression earnest. "Becky, I don't ever want to be so far away from you again. Living apart isn't working for us. It never has."

My heart skipped a beat as he continued, "I put in a bid on my old house, and the owner agreed to sell it to me. It'll be ready for me to move in at the end of June."

A surge of happiness at the implication washed over me. He was moving back! And into the house I'd always wished I'd lived in. I beamed. "I bet your family is thrilled! I know I am."

He frowned. "About that ... I, uh ... haven't told them yet."

I had to ask, "Why?"

He looked down, averting his gaze, his voice filled with vulnerability. "I wanted to be sure first. And now that I am, I want to ask you something." He paused, his eyes searching mine.

"Anything." I held my breath.

He reached into his pocket and pulled out a gold ring with

a tiny diamond solitaire. "Will you give a real chance to a relationship between us now?"

I gasped. In his hand was the promise ring that had been
taken from me just hours after he'd slid it onto my finger.
"Where did you find that?"

Confusion clouded his eyes, then hope. "You don't know?'

I shook my head fervently.

"You ... You didn't bury it?"

"*Bury* it?" What was he talking about?

He wore the saddest expression.

"No!" I cried, rushing to explain what I knew. Which
wasn't much. He must have thought me heartless all these
years! "Dad—*Dirk*—ripped it off my finger when I got home
that last night we were together. I never saw it again. Mom
came out of her room to see what the yelling was about, and
that's when he shoved her. She—she lost her balance and—"

He stared at me for a beat. I hadn't wanted to tell him this
part because I knew he'd try to accept the blame for my mother's accident.

I rushed on before he could interject. "I had thirty minutes
to throw everything important to me in a bag. Child protective
services came to get me the next morning when the cops came
back to arrest him—the doctors sent them. Mrs. Palmer saw
me leaving and demanded they let me use her suitcase. I still
have it. Anyway, before the cops took him away, the man I'd
thought was my father said—he said he'd find a way to hurt
you if I didn't forget about you. So I tried." I sobbed. "I really
tried." I crumpled into his waiting arms. "He knew people
everywhere, and I was so naive. I didn't want you or your
family to get hurt because of me. I sent you that email because
I was afraid for you. And then I disappeared. I'm so sorry."

He held me tight, and I clung to him. "I wish even more that I'd never left. When my dad told me about his new job in Providence, I asked if I could stay here, but my mother was heartbroken I would even ask. So we compromised. She promised, only four years, then I could do what I wanted. You and I still had summers and vacations. And that last summer ... Making plans to go to URI together. We were so close to slaying your dragon and breaking you free that I could taste it. And then, you were gone." He pulled away and held my tear-streaked face in his hands. "I would have been there for you. I *wanted* to be there for you. I tried everything to find you. And when I realized you were hiding on purpose ..." His voice cracked with emotion so raw, it broke me.

"I'm so sorry." There wasn't anything more to say. My list of regrets stretched to the moon.

He tipped my chin up with his finger and fixed his steel-gray eyes on mine. "I never want to lose you again."

"I don't want to lose you again, either." My voice cracked under the weight of the admission. I knew it in my heart, but I hadn't said it out loud.

"Will you promise? Will you wear the ring?" he asked again.

I nodded. "But ... on a chain, around my neck. Just in case. I—I'll be heartbroken enough if this doesn't work out. I don't want to have to explain to everyone—"

"I understand. But I'm going to prove you wrong, I swear it." He pressed his lips to mine, sealing his vow. My heart was full of love for this incredible man standing before me.

"'Til June, then. Our secret."

"Our secret."

Our lips met again in a sweet, lingering kiss. All my

worries melted away, leaving only the certainty that love had brought us back together on this Valentine's Day, and it was a love that would endure, no matter the distance or the challenges that lay ahead.

"I still have the photo album you made me," I said, as if that could make up for anything.

He kissed me again and then whispered against my lips, "I love you, Valentine. You were always my Valentine, and you'll always *be* my Valentine."

"I love you, too." I snuggled into him, and he kissed me like he never wanted to stop.

Our new chapter had begun.

CHAPTER 15

## Liam

I flew home a few days later, and the weeks became an endless blend of longing and excitement, the kind that lingers in the heart like the sweet memory of a stolen kiss. I missed Becky like my drawing compass without its pencil, and every night, I'd find myself alone in my thoughts, wishing I was back in Colorado, snuggling up by a fire with her, keeping each other warm on these cold winter nights and planning our future together.

But I was on the east coast, far from the Rockies, in a drafty apartment that was empty without her laughter and cold without her warmth. The promises we'd made to each other felt fragile yet steadfast, like a delicate web spun by a skillful spider: strong and secure but easily destroyed by the brush of an opposing force.

By April, I was missing her almost more than I could bear. I was also more than ready to quit my job. The nonsense with my boss had escalated when we lost an important contract after he had insisted on cutting corners again.

An idea suddenly came to me. I scooped up my phone

from the kitchen counter and scrolled until I found the number of the Elk Creek Falls Realtor I'd been working with.

"Elk Creek Realty. Hello, Liam." Her warm, friendly voice was one of the things I liked most about her. That, and her knowledge of the area and promise to be discreet. During our first conversation, I discovered she knew my entire family.

But then again, who in the Colorado Springs area didn't?

"Hi, Dawn," I replied, my voice wavering with anticipation. "I was wondering ... Do you know if the property next door is for sale?" The lot had been bulldozed after the fire and had been sitting empty for months.

"I can check on that for you. Anything else?"

"Have there been any updates on the family living there? Any chance they'll be out sooner than June?"

She sighed. "No. Remember? They're waiting until the end of the school year to make the transition easier for their kids."

An all-too familiar story. "I understand that. I do. I just ... I ..."

"You want to get out here ASAP to get life started with your Becky. I can't blame you. How about I look for a temporary rental?"

It was tempting. But I liked staying at the inn when I visited, and I knew my family would be hurt if I rented a place instead of staying with any of them.

"No," I replied. "But thank you. I can stay with family."

Except for one small thing: My family still had no idea of my plans. And I wasn't planning to tell them until I closed on the house.

But the house was just one piece of the puzzle. The other piece was for me and Becky to fill every corner of it and the lot next door with love and laughter, just as I remembered from my childhood.

For now, I could work on that other piece.

The next morning, I searched job sites for open positions around Colorado Springs, hoping to find an architectural position that would allow me to move sooner than June. But no one seemed to be hiring.

It was as if the universe itself was testing my resolve. As I stared at the computer screen, I pondered the idea of freelancing and starting my own business. The thought was both thrilling and terrifying. Though I was confident in my design skills, I didn't know anything about starting a business.

But Becky and her dad did.

Could I do it?

It would be risky. But for her, I was willing to take the leap.

With newfound determination, I researched the steps required to set up my own business. It was daunting, but the thought of being closer to her sooner drove me. Caffeine and adrenaline were my fuel through the night, and when the sun began to rise over the river, bathing the water in ribbons of majestic color, I was glad it was Saturday and I didn't have to be anywhere.

There was a third piece. I wanted to do one more thing before I caught up on my sleep.

In the search engine, I typed *fine jewelers in Colorado Springs*.

This final piece would symbolize my promise to love Becky unconditionally, no matter the distance or obstacles we faced, and ensure that she knew I'd always keep my promises. I wanted it to be as unique and beautiful as the love we shared, a constant reminder of the future we were building together.

As I clicked through various designs and settings, my

excitement grew. This ring would hold the power to bring us closer, to bind us officially, contractually, in a way the promise ring hadn't.

It would remind us that these new promises were for forever.

When I found what I was looking for, I called Brenna.

"What was so important you couldn't text?" she answered breathlessly.

"What, you busy or something?" I thought I could hear Brendan in the background.

Interesting ...

"Yes?" It was more of a question. "I was in the loft."

"Go back up there—alone. This is a secret."

"Okaaaay."

"You alone now?" I know I sounded anxious, but this was important.

"I am. So, what have you got for me?"

"An aquamarine eternity ring with a diamond solitaire," I stated evenly.

"Ew, cuz. No, I will *not* marry you."

"Ha ha." I filled her in, and she squealed.

"Shh! I don't want Becky to suspect anything."

"No worries. She and her dad went to the lumber store. It's just me and Brendan here."

"Uh-huh ..."

"Shut it."

I laughed. "Can you use your super Brenna powers to find out Becky's ring size?"

"Which finger?"

I rolled my eyes. "Seriously?"

"I've got to be sure. She's my friend, you know. This is serious."

"It is. Can you also pick it up for me?"

"Of course! When do you plan to—"

"I'm not sure yet. And *please* don't tell anyone. Not even Gran. We're keeping our relationship a secret for now, until I can move back."

She snorted. "Worst-kept secret in the history of worst-kept secrets."

I sighed. "Thanks, Bren."

# CHAPTER 16

# *Beck*

D ad and I sat on either side of Mom in the pre-op area, waiting for transport to take her to the operating room. A thin hospital-issued blanket covered her frail form. In her eyes, a mixture of hope and trepidation swirled, and she nibbled on her lower lip. Dad clutched his mother's rosary, praying over her in Spanish for the miracle that would restore the use of her legs.

Silently, I prayed for an additional miracle.

When she woke up in the hospital after her accident, Mom had been unable to speak, a cruel mystery that had left her silent all these years. Countless doctors and specialists had examined her, yet none could find the cause of her muteness.

Mom's fingers clutched the small whiteboard, one of many we'd become so accustomed to and dependent upon over the years. When Dad finished his prayer, she picked up her marker and scribbled a message in haste, her usually steady hand now shaky.

*I need you to know the truth,* she wrote. She caught my gaze and locked her eyes to mine. The gravity of her expression made my own spine tingle.

I swallowed hard, my heart pounding in my chest as her blue eyes pierced mine. What truth? I thought I knew all the secrets she'd carried.

I nodded, urging her to continue.

She took a deep breath, her hands trembling as she wrote. *You weren't born early.*

I'd wondered about that when I met my real father. Throughout my childhood, every time I messed up, missed a milestone, got a bad grade, bloomed later than the other girls, or didn't understand something, my early birth had been the proposed cause.

The story was that I'd experienced growth and learning delays and had fine motor issues in my early years. My mind raced, wondering if my development had been purposefully sabotaged to perpetuate the lie.

My mother's eyes glistened with tears, and she continued to write. *I'm sorry, Becky. We—my parents and I—told that story to protect you.*

Protect me? From what?

Or who? If it was a who, I understood why they did it, though it still hurt.

She went on to explain, her writing wobbly but determined, detailing how her parents had reacted to her pregnancy news and set about finding her a husband STAT. My birth had been a consequence of a love that defied their plans for her and would have brought shame to their family if the secret of her unwed status had leaked. They gave her a choice: If she wanted to keep me, she had to marry Dirk.

As I read, the pieces of the puzzle began to fall into place.

My mother had been deeply in love with my father. My grandparents did not approve of him, which Dad had told me. After they broke up and he left, she'd been forced into marrying Dirk, the son of their closest friends, a man who had proposed to her several times and been turned down. He hadn't been told about the child she carried.

To hide the truth, Mom's parents had concocted the story of an early birth to quell any suspicions about my true parentage. They even went so far as to limit Mom's calorie intake so that I'd be born underweight.

I was horrified that anyone could treat their child that way and was glad they were no longer around to continue to hurt her. As a child, I hated visiting them. Aloof and cold, they'd never shown affection toward me—or anyone. Tears streamed down my face as Dad and I both reached out and gently squeezed her hands, assuring her of our support and forgiveness, silently acknowledging the love that bound us together, a love that had endured even in the face of deception.

The pain in my dad's face was just as anguishing to witness. To not know that he had a daughter for *seventeen years*. To forgive Mom so completely and unconditionally. I didn't know if I could do that had I been in his shoes. I was still harboring some anger and resentment for my childhood and the loss of seventeen years with a father who would have loved me completely and unconditionally.

A flicker of hope in her eyes expressed her relief at my forgiveness. I loved her so much, and I hated that she lived with guilt from a time when she thought she was doing what was best for us.

This surgery, while we hoped for it to be a success, had the potential to not only restore her physical abilities and personal freedoms but also mend the broken bonds of our family. Give our little unit a fresh start.

When they wheeled her away, Mom's gaze locked onto mine until she disappeared from view. As I sat in the waiting room, my thoughts swirled like the caramel sauce on Xavier's toffee coffee, now a must-have for him on game days. I clung to the hope that Mom's voice, long silenced, would soon find its way back to us, and that together, we would retell the story of our lives with honesty, love, and forgiveness.

# CHAPTER 17

*Liam*

Cathy Monroe's surgery was a success. Becky called every day, updating me on her progress and milestones. Once the swelling subsided, she began to blow through the doctors' expected timelines, literally a walking miracle, though it would take considerable time before she was able to build up enough strength to walk unassisted.

Her voice, however, hadn't returned, but Becky still held out hope that since there wasn't a clear medical reason, love and prayer would restore it one day.

One weeknight in early May, I found myself still at work but not working. For the last couple of hours, I'd been occupied by a personal project. On the drafting table were the blueprints of my childhood home. I had quite a few ideas for updating the layout without losing the best parts from my childhood, as well as plans for the lot next door, which I'd made an official offer on.

When my phone vibrated on the desk, I glanced at the caller ID, and my heart kicked up a beat.

It was Becky.

Becky, the brilliant craftswoman who brought old struc-
tures to life with her unwavering passion for making old
things new again. She'd taken Brenna's vision and my designs
and transformed the old family barn into the wedding venue
of my cousin's dreams, a stunning and warm space where
countless love stories would unfold under its protective
embrace.

Maybe our love story, too.

I answered with a smile, taking in every detail of the face
that had lived in my heart and in my dreams since I first saw
it. The face that I wanted to look at every day for the rest of
my life. "Hey, beautiful. What's up?"

Her voice, usually filled with boundless enthusiasm,
carried a hint of worry, betraying her even expression. "Willy,
we've got a problem. Possibly a big one."

Concern gripped me like the cold fingertips of an ice fisher.
"What happened? Tell me."

She explained that the final inspection was scheduled for
tomorrow and the electrician had noticed something off. He'd
found a crack in a beam, and the wood had shifted. She
needed my expertise to assess the situation and determine if
there was a structure issue. Her father didn't think so, but
they wanted me to do that math and make sure it was sound.

"I don't know how this happened," she said. "It was
perfect when it was set in. How can something shift like
that?"

"Hey, it's going to be okay," I reassured her. "Wood swells
and shrinks, especially at the change of season. Send me some
pictures so I can see what's going on. We'll figure this out
together."

My phone chimed with incoming images. I saw the

problem right away, and I was one hundred percent certain humidity had caused the wood to swell, resulting in its slight shift and subsequent hairline crack. Purely cosmetic, it was unlikely to even be noticed by anyone who wasn't looking for it.

I asked for measurements. Becky had them ready. Despite the visual chaos and her fear that she'd messed up big time, her voice was steady, cool, and professional.

With a deep breath, I analyzed the photos and measurements carefully. It was sturdy and set; there wasn't anything to fix unless they wanted to replace the entire piece.

"Becky," I said, my voice steady as I tried to project professionalism and confidence to assuage her fears, "I've reviewed the pictures and measurements. Done the math. It's off, and there's a small crack, but the structure is sound. The imperfection is purely cosmetic."

Her relief came in a whoosh of a long breath. "Oh, thank goodness. You have no idea how worried I was. Now I'm just bummed that it's not perfect."

Maybe I shouldn't have used *imperfection*. "It's got character now," I replied. Her snort made me smile. "Hey, I'm booking a flight for tonight. I'll be there by tomorrow morning to assess everything in person and to stand by your side during the inspection."

"You don't need to—"

"I *want* to." There was a chance the inspector wouldn't agree with my assessment. I had to be there to make sure there was no doubt in his mind that the structure was secure. We were a team, on this project and in life and love, even if we hadn't said it out loud yet. I would move the Rockies themselves to ensure this project—and all the dreams we'd shared when we were younger, plus new ones, came to fruition.

After the call, I looked around my office, my thoughts consumed by the challenges that lay ahead. Not just for the barn inspection but also proving that love and determination could conquer any obstacle.

I booked my flight and packed up to go home. Tomorrow, I would be by Becky's side, where I belonged, ready to testify that the barn, like our love, could weather any challenge.

# CHAPTER 18

## *Beck*

The early afternoon sun bathed the newly renovated barn in a warm, golden light. As I stood there, my nerves wobbled like the water in my level tool. The air was filled with anticipation and the scent of fresh wood, a reminder of the countless hours Dad and I and our hired crews and volunteers had spent inside renovating this old structure. Beside me, Brenna fidgeted, scribbling away in one of her notebooks.

Willy flashed me an encouraging smile. My dad stood nearby, his face lined with pride, a silent testament to the father-daughter bond that we shared.

We were all gathered here for the pivotal moment—the final inspection. Kingston and Jackson Brewer would marry the Ranford sisters in a double wedding in this very barn in just a few weeks. We needed the inspector's approval today to proceed with our timeline of finishing tasks like loading in the tables, chairs, dais, and all the things that fancy parties required.

The inspector arrived, right on time, a balding man of

short stature and no-nonsense demeanor. I introduced him to our small, anxious group, and he nodded politely.

Willy stepped forward, his voice steady as he addressed the inspector. "There's one issue we want to bring to your attention," he began, gesturing toward a particular beam that caught his discerning eye. "It's at a slight angle, and there's a hairline crack, but rest assured, it's structurally sound."

He explained away the defects, providing details to support his conclusion that the issue was cosmetic. The inspector listened attentively, making notes on his electronic tablet. I held my breath, hoping Willy's honesty and expertise would be favorable.

A few minutes later, the official inspection began. Every moment felt like an eternity as the inspector meticulously checked the structure from top to bottom. The first floor was scrutinized and every detail assessed with a critical eye. Then, with careful steps, he ascended the iron spiral staircase to the loft, where Brenna had her office, a cozy seating area, and a kitchenette.

The minutes passed in tense silence. I glanced at Brenna. She was moments away from her beloved barn becoming an official, licensed wedding venue. To her, the barn wasn't just a structure; it was a place where love would bloom for couples beginning their happily-ever-afters.

Just as the tension seemed unbearable, a cheerful voice echoed from behind us. "Hey, guys. Hey, Bren-naa!"

We turned to see Brendan walking toward us with a wide grin. His arrival was a surprise, as he was supposed to be playing with the Volts in Madison tonight.

Brenna's eyes lit up with surprise. "Bren-dan! I thought you were out of town."

He chuckled, his eyes sparkling with excitement. "Change of plans! Got my NHL call-up, so I'm playing with the Edge in Denver tonight instead. And then I thought, where do I most want to be with my unexpected afternoon off? It was a no-brainer."

Willy clapped Brendan on the back. "That's incredible, man! Congratulations!"

Brenna beamed, her happiness radiating like a beacon. "I can't believe it! This is amazing news. Good luck tonight."

"You should come watch me play." He waggled his eyebrows flirtatiously.

I whispered in her ear. "Ooooh. I think he liiiikes you."

"He flirts with everybody," she mumbled out the corner of her mouth.

"Who said anything about flirting?" I whispered back.

She shot me a glare, and I laughed.

As Brendan regaled us with stats about the Edge and the New Orleans Crescents, tonight's opponent, the inspector reappeared. His expression gave nothing away, and he delivered his verdict with a calm, professional tone, telling Brenna that the barn had passed inspection.

"Yes!" Brendan whooped. He reached for Brenna and scooped her up, twirling her in a circle while she squealed in protest. "Big day for both of us, Bren-naa!"

"Put me *down!*"

He set her on the floor with a roguish grin, and she made a show of smoothing out invisible wrinkles in her shirt before turning back to the inspector, who'd watched the show of affection with amused interest.

Brenna reached out to shake his hand, gratitude shining in

her eyes. "Thank you so much! You have no idea how much this means to me."

The inspector left, and I wrapped Brenna in a tight hug. "I'm so happy for you! This barn is going to be perfect for the weddings. I can't wait to see the pictures of Kingston and Jackson's weddings."

Brenna's eyes twinkled mischievously as she glanced at Willy. "Pictures? Aren't you coming with Liam?"

He cleared his throat, his cheeks tinged with a faint blush. "Actually, I was planning to ask Becky—*Beck*—after the inspection. Just got the invitation this week, you know."

Brenna rolled her eyes. "You've known about the weddings for months. You should've asked sooner. What if she had plans?"

I glanced at him, and before he could speak, I smiled. "I might be free," I said, my heart dancing with excitement at the prospect of being his date. As far as they knew, we weren't even dating so ...

Willy grinned, a mixture of relief and adoration in his eyes. "Well, in that case, Becky, would you do me the honor of being my date to my cousins' weddings?"

I nodded. "Of course. I'd love to."

Brenna shot me a knowing look, and I decided not to dwell on why he had waited to ask me. It wasn't important. What mattered was that we would be together, celebrating love and new beginnings in the barn we had all poured our time and hearts into.

"We should celebrate," he whispered softly into my ear. "Dinner tonight?"

I shivered. I still hadn't gotten used to the low rumble of his grownup baritone.

"Yes," I replied, turning my head so the others wouldn't see my burning cheeks. "What time?"

"Now?" he asked. "We could go for a walk along the creek first."

"Yes. Okay." Walking along the creek and smooching on a particular swinging bench had been one of our favorite pastimes when we were younger.

We said goodbye to everyone, and I hugged my dad, who was on his way to visit Mom. Since her surgery, I'd hardly seen him. Every spare moment he had was spent with Mom.

Once outside, Willy reached for my hand. We laced our fingers together, and I smiled up at him. He grinned widely, and I felt the pulse in his thumb kick up.

I got the feeling he had more than dinner and a walk on his mind.

CHAPTER 19

## Liam

The western sun cast a warm glow over downtown Palmer City as it started its descent behind the mountains. I savored every moment, holding my secret plan close.

We'd left my car at the inn and strolled along the gentle curve of the Creek Walk, just as we had countless times in our younger years. Leisurely ambling, hands laced together, neither of us in a rush, as if we could somehow stall the minutes, slowing time to stretch out our evening together.

After dinner at The Olde Train Station Ristorante—it had become our go-to grownup spot—and dessert at Crepe Suzette's, my nerves kicked up with anticipation as we retraced our steps back to the inn. In the dim light of the streetlamps, I stole glances at Becky. A few times she caught me and squeezed my hand. Her smile, her laugh, the way her eyes sparkled … I wanted to record every bit of it in my mind to play over and over again during the weeks ahead when we had to be apart.

The car ride was quiet until I missed the turn for her street.

"Where are we going?" she asked.

"The new barn. If that's okay? There's something I need to do there. And I'm not ready to bring you home yet. Want to come along?"

"Of course. I'm not ready to go home." She stretched across the console and placed a soft kiss on my cheek. I turned my head to meet her lips.

"Willy," she laughed, pulling away. "Eyes on the road!"

I laughed and turned onto the dirt road that traversed my family's property. Thank goodness it was only a short drive. I thought I was going to burst.

I parked in front of the barn and raced around the car to open her door. She took my hand and smiled as she stood up and I pulled her to me for a long, slow kiss.

"I like kissing you," she stated, holding my face in her hands. "I'll never tire of it."

"Good." I pulled away. "More later, then. Follow me?"

She nodded, and I held her hand tight, my heart hammering in my chest, every beat urging me on.

Swiftie whinnied hello as we entered. The other horses—Old Mr. Cuthbert, Chocolate Powder (two guesses who named him, ha ha), and Jewel—echoed his greeting as Becky went straight to his stall.

"Oh you sweet horse," Becky cooed, reaching into the bag tacked to the outside of the stall. "What the—there's something mixed in here ..."

"There is?" I asked, raising an eyebrow and willing myself to stay cool.

"Yes, it's—OH!" In her palm, she held the small black velvet box I'd hidden there before the inspection.

I plucked it from her palm and dropped to one knee. My

hand trembled as I popped open the lid, revealing the diamond solitaire and aquamarine eternity band.

My body may have shaken a little, but my voice was steady. "Becky, I've loved you as long as I've known you." I swallowed. I had so much more to say. *Get it together, Brewer.*

She lowered herself onto her knees and rested her hands on them. Her eyes locked on mine.

I took a deep breath. "Your quiet strength, your physical and emotional strength ... What you've endured would have broken most people. But you patch the cracks, layer on some new paint, and push on, with your glass more than half full and still yourself underneath it all. There's no one who awes me more than you, no one I admire more than you, no one I want to be with more than you." Behind me, Swiftie snorted. I smirked. "Not even you, boy. Sorry."

He answered me with a whinny, and Becky laughed.

I dropped my gaze to the open box. "The band has a single stone for all the years I've loved you."

She let out a soft gasp, and her mouth dropped open in surprise.

I took another deep, fortifying breath before I asked the question that seared within me like a cattle brand, the question I'd wanted to ask her for two decades. "Becky, we belong together. We've always known it. Can we make it official? Will you marry me?"

I winced. Not the exact words I wanted to use. My nerves had gotten the better of me, and I'd skipped over some of the points I wanted to share.

But her eyes shimmered with emotion, and she spoke the one word, that one single word that held the power to shape our future. It hung in the air. "Yes."

I slipped the diamond ring onto her finger, and she threw her arms around me. We shared a kiss, but then she pulled away, wiping at the tears that had fallen down her cheeks.

"I love you so much, Willy. I regret breaking up with you and disappearing. More than you could ever know. We lost so much time because I was scared and I thought you'd be better off without me. What I did hurt us both, and I'm so sorry. I don't want to waste any more time."

My heart cracked under the weight of her perceived guilt. "You were just a kid. No one can blame you for anything you did to protect yourself or anyone you loved."

She sat back on her knees and lifted her chin. "I grew up, though. And I stayed hidden. Out of touch. On purpose. We lost so much time because of me. We could have been together and happy all those years, just like we planned."

"It's okay," I assured her. "We're together now."

"We are. And I can't stand the thought of a long engagement," she confessed, soft and earnest. "Your Uncle Quinn is a Justice of the Peace. The barn will be beautifully decorated the morning of the rehearsal dinner ... Let's get married then, in *our* barn. And we can honeymoon in Rhode Island under the guise of packing you up and tell everyone else when we get back. You know how those Gilded Age mansions are still on my bucket list. What do you think?"

A grin spread across my face as I considered the idea. The thought of making the old barn, our sanctuary, the beginning of our forever, where we'd made and built so many memories, hit me right in heart. There couldn't be a more perfect idea. "I think Brenna will freak."

"Then we won't tell her." Her eyes glinted with love and a side of mischief. "And I don't want to take away from your cousins, so ... Let's just have our parents there while Brenna and the wedding parties are getting their hair and nails done and all those other things couples do the morning of big weddings."

It was a brilliant idea. "Let's do it. I'll handle everything. You just get a dress."

Her face glowed with excitement, and she leaned toward me. I dropped the box and kissed her with fervor, sealing this new promise, wanting her to feel everything I was feeling. My thoughts raced to the future and when I would return to Palmer City and this barn—for good.

"The next time I come here, it'll be to stay," I said.

With a tender smile, Becky whispered, "I'm counting the days."

And so was I.

# Shining Star Barn Events
*Brenna's To-Do List*

## Who: <u>Ranford-Brewer Wedding Squared</u>
## When: <u>June</u>

## 1 Month Before—*May*
   √ *Inspection (DO NOT let nerves manifest into a Cheshire cat grin!)*
   √ *Load in all the things (Ask Brendan to assemble Volts Volunteer Crew)*

## 2 Weeks Before—*June 1*
   √ *Finalize EVERYTHING*
   √ *Start decorating*

## 1 Week Before—*see list on tablet*

*Notes:*
*\*~~Liam can't travel until Thanksgiving.~~*
*\*~~Beck's business license is still waiting on approval.~~*
*~~Vibe: Neither seem to feel the urgency (to get together). C'mon, people!~~*
*\*~~Talk to Aunt Patricia about using her box at the arena for a "family"~~*
*~~Valentine's Day outing. Get Liam and Beck to attend~~* <u>~~BY ANY MEANS~~</u>
<u>~~NECESSARY.~~</u> *~~Maybe for a "progress check?"~~*
*\*Is there time to construct a gazebo?*
*\*Investigate why Liam is looking so smug*
*\*Liam & Beck Project #2: A separate structure for future brides and their attendants.*

# CHAPTER 20

*Beck*

T he barn, dressed in its rustic charm and adorned with twinkle lights, stood as a testament to our journey together. Inside, the scent of just-delivered fresh flowers intermingled with the earthy aroma of weathered wood and new stain, a heady scent that had me wondering if we could find a way to capture it and market it as a scented candle. "Barn Wedding" would surely be a bestseller.

For the last six months, we'd worked together with my dad and Brenna to transform it into the perfect wedding venue. Once it was our old sanctuary, this tranquil place where I'd always felt safe and secure. Now it would be the start of our happily-ever-after.

I stared at myself in the full-length mirror. I'd chosen a sheer overlay halter-style gown with a fit-and flare silhouette. It was modest but hugged my curves and accentuated my waist. Layers of ivory chiffon and antique lace added a romantic touch.

Downstairs, Willy, his parents, my mom, and his Uncle Quinn waited for me and Dad to start the ceremony. I couldn't see them from inside Brenna's loft office, so my dad described everything below as he adjusted my veil and waited for the cue to start.

"Quinn's all set to go on the dais with Liam and his father. Your moms are sitting in the fancy chairs from the sweetheart table at the base of the stairs." He grinned and stretched out his arms for a hug. "They're all ready when you are."

I hugged him tightly, grateful to have him here and in my life. "I love you, Dad."

"I love you too, amorcito. Now go get married so I can marry your mom next."

"What?!" I pulled out of his embrace, not sure I'd heard him correctly.

He chuckled. "Oops. Pretend you are surprised, okay? Your mother didn't want to overshadow your moment with our news."

"That's impossible." I shook my head and hugged him again. "Oh, Dad. Do it. Do it today. While Quinn is here. You can get a license later, right?"

He shrugged. "I don't know. So it's good that we already have the license, yes?"

I squealed. "Yes!"

"Shh!" he leaned to whisper in my ear. "You're not supposed to know, remember?"

"Right!"

The instrumental version of Taylor Swift's "Love Story" filtered up from below us. "That's my cue," he said. He picked up my bouquet of wildflowers and peonies. "You sure you want to carry these down that thing?"

"I'm sure. It's a very sturdy staircase. You installed it your-self," I reminded him.

He scrunched his nose. "It is not the staircase that worries me."

I snorted. "I'll see you at the bottom. Go!"

Laughing, he placed a kiss on the top of my head and handed me the flowers. "Yes, boss."

My heart raced, nerves and excitement mingling as I descended the spiral iron staircase. With each turn, I locked eyes with Willy and smiled wider. At the bottom, I slipped my arm through Dad's. The short walk to the dais and up the steps seemed to take forever.

Dad let go at the base of the stairs, and I took my place next to Willy, my hand finding its natural fit within his. This was our moment.

Quinn's voice projected joy and warmth. "Who gives this woman to this man in holy matrimony?"

"We do."

I gasped and whirled around. My mother, whose voice had been silent for almost ten long years, had *spoken*. And she was standing, leaning on Dad! It was a moment of pure magic, an unexpected and much-prayed-for miracle that swelled my heart and clogged my throat with a lump so big, I didn't know how I was going to recite my vows.

I couldn't contain my joy and disbelief. With tears streaming down my cheeks, I handed Willy my bouquet and hurried down the steps, throwing my arms around my mother. Dad wrapped his arms around both of us. We were a whirl-wind of sobs, laughter, and love—a family made whole.

"Go," she whispered. Her voice was hoarse and choppy, but—it was *her voice!* I'd almost forgotten what it sounded like. Fresh tears waterfalled down my face, and she dabbed at them with the tissues in her hand.

I kissed her cheek "I love you so much, Mom. This is the best day ever!"

Dad winked as if to say, *You just wait,* and I laughed again.

I returned to the stage and reclaimed my flowers. Quinn continued the ceremony, moved by the miracle we'd just witnessed and wiping his eyes as he read his lines. His voice was a soothing balm, calming to our overexcited hearts. Willy and I exchanged vows, promises that honored our past, celebrated our present, and inspired our future. Then the rings, and the kiss.

*The kiss.*

I didn't know what came over him, other than extreme happiness. Willy, never the showman except on his blueprints, held me, dipped me, and kissed me so thoroughly and scandalously I swore my whole body blushed red. A kiss that was filled with all the dreams we'd woven together and all the love that had brought us to this moment.

Quinn pronounced us husband and wife, and we kissed again. Just because we could. Then I hastily whispered Dad's plan into Willy's ear. I was sure he wouldn't mind, but I thought it courteous to fill him in.

"Of course. That's amazing!" he said, squeezing me to him.

"Two dreams of mine fulfilled in one perfect morning," I said. I turned toward my dad, and he nodded, bending over to whisper in Mom's ears. She glanced at me with a worried look, and I grinned back when I saw her lips mouth *yes.*

Dad beamed and addressed our little group. "If you all have a few more moments to spare, Cathy and I would also like to be married today. Quinn? Can we move up our timeline? We don't want to wait until the kids get back from their honeymoon to do this."

"Can't blame you for that," he teased.

Dad helped Mom to her feet again, and I handed my bouquet to her. They kept it short, and as Dad pulled the rings from his pocket, I couldn't help but wonder if this had been his plan all along. I couldn't blame him, either. He'd waited almost twenty-seven years for this.

After the ceremonies, Willy drove us to the Realtor's office in Elk Creek Falls. There, we closed on his childhood home and the lot next door, a place we would rebuild with new, happy memories that would become our new sanctuary. I couldn't wait to embark on our new adventure—together, making the house our home, build our workshops next door and fill both with love, laughter, and the promises of a lifetime.

We might have grown up to become Liam and Beck, but we'd always be Willy and Becky underneath. And we were more than ready to finally embrace the joy and love that awaited us in the weeks and years ahead. Our hearts were entwined, and our future held a promise as strong and enduring as the beams that supported the old barn—unyielding, steadfast, and full of love.

# Epilogue
## LIAM

The soft early morning light filtered through the gauzy curtains in my—our—suite at the Creekside Inn, rousing me from my favorite dream. I kept my eyes closed, not wanting it to end. It felt so real this time. And I was warm. So warm. Unusually warm for June in Colorado.

"Good morning, husband."

Husband?

My eyes snapped open. Next to me, in my arms, was the source of the warmth. Becky's eyes were half open, and her lazy smile just begged to be kissed. The even rise and fall of her breathing soothed my soul.

"Good morning, wifey." Her soft giggling made me feel even warmer. From my position spooning her, I couldn't reach her lips. Probably for the best. Morning breath and all that. Instead, I leaned in and brushed my lips along the nape of her neck.

She sighed contentedly. "I suppose we should get out of bed? The first ceremony is in a couple hours."

I nuzzled my face between her ear and shoulder. "Five more minutes."

"Ten."

"Deal."

She turned to face me, and we just gazed at each other, not moving or saying a word. Not needing to. Everything we needed to communicate was right there, in each other's eyes.

More than ten minutes later, we reluctantly rose and readied for Jackson and Kingston's weddings. I grinned as I opened the sock drawer. On the dresser were handmade cards from the Warner girls and two teddy bears dressed as a bride and groom—on loan of course. We'd had to swear them to secrecy yesterday afternoon, and I was pleasantly surprised—and a little disappointed—with their lack of shenanigans when we returned from the rehearsal dinner last night.

We'd decided to play it cool and keep up our charade of a secret relationship. We knew we weren't fooling anyone, but we didn't want to take any attention from the brides and grooms. And it was kind of fun to know they had no idea about our biggest secret.

I locked up our rings securely in the room's safe, hiding them away like a secret treasure, and we exited the room onto the veranda hand in hand. Becky reached for me, and I couldn't resist another kiss on the way to my car.

I heard the click of the latch to the unit next door opening, and it took a second to register that we weren't alone.

"Sorry, Liam!" Bailey Dexter apologized. I'd met her during a previous stay, and we knew a lot of the same people. "Don't want to interrupt, but ... you're blocking the stairs."

"Sorry, Bailey." I noticed she was dressed fancy for a

Saturday morning. Her brother Jason was the Voltage's goalie, and he was one of Kingston's groomsmen. "Are you going to the weddings, too?"

"I am." She glanced at Becky and smiled. "I didn't know you two were official. Finally!"

"Uh ..."

"We're keeping it a secret for now," Becky said. "So ..."

"My lips are sealed!" She grinned as she scooted around us. "See you there!"

"See you there," I echoed. We watched her go and then burst out laughing.

"Let's go, husband." Becky lifted on her toes for a kiss, and I was happy to oblige.

I'd never been to a double wedding before. Well, except for my own. But not a daylong thing. Brenna was the pro everyone expected her to be, moving us guests seamlessly from one thing to the next, from Jackson and Chelsea's wedding to lunch, then Kingston and Taylor's wedding to dinner, and now the ultimate party. The barn was near to bursting with family, friends, and hockey players. My heart beat a little faster when I saw Bailey chatting with Lawson. She winked at us and I grinned back, knowing our secret was safe with her.

One Volt in particular almost stole the show from the newlyweds. Brendan was in rare form, unleashing every cheesy dance move in the history of dance moves, no doubt trying to impress Brenna. Her bemused headshakes and efforts not to laugh only fueled his determination, and when the music slowed, I was happy to see her accept his invitation to dance.

Becky and I held each other close during the slow songs, deciding we didn't care what people thought. They'd know soon enough just how official we were. We whispered ideas for our honeymoon trip to Newport. I couldn't wait to pack up my apartment, start our new life together in Palmer City, and build new memories on top of our old ones.

The road ahead was open, and we were ready for every adventure along the way, together, finally, forever.

THANKS FOR READING *Keep Me in Mind!* If you loved it, please leave a review and share with your sweetrom-loving friends!

**All of Brenna's brothers and cousins will get their own stories soon! Keegan's is up next. Look for *One Margarita,* Book 1 in the new Brewer Brides series!**

KEEGAN BREWER'S life is perfectly fine. He's content with his perfected daily routine: early mornings dreaming up new craft beers for his family's restaurant, afternoons managing Brewski's from behind the scenes, and evenings syncing Christmas songs to the LED light display on and around his tiny caboose home on his grandparents' ranchland. Sure, it irks him that his favorite retired hockey player is opening a rival restaurant across the street, and he'll defend his family's business no matter what it takes. One thing he knows for sure is that he wants nothing to do with the bombshell blonde who wants his brewery secrets to make her dad's restaurant a success.

Daughter of a hockey legend, heiress to a billion-dollar sports equipment and fashion empire, and Olympic champion in her own right, Astoria Kubek practically grew up at Brewski's. A lifetime ago, she and the Brewer kids were friends, on and off the ice, playing peewee hockey and pranking the pros. She's been tasked with creating a signature brew to put their new family restaurant on the map. And she wants Keegan's help.

It'll take everything she's got to get the grumpy brewer's attention, never mind his assistance. But the man won't even look at her. Astoria is used to winning, but winning Keegan over becomes more than a job—especially when she discovers the power of his dimples and his adoration of her crazy foster kitten. Making him smile is her new mission, even if her messy life gives him hives. She'll do whatever it takes to bring him true Christmas joy—including unleashing her adorable kitty as a secret weapon.

Together, can they craft a perfect beer and gift each other with the most special Christmas gift of all?

*One Margarita is a sweet enemies-to-more grumpy-sunshine workplace romance with heartwarming characters, small-town shenanigans, and the Fluffiest Furball in the West.*

*Read the Palmer City Voltage series, where it all began!*

*Love on the Ice*
Alexei & Ginny

*Cruising on Ice*
Kingston & Taylor

*Christmas on Ice*
Trask & Kami

*Melting the Ice*
Zander & Gemma

*Sparks on the Ice*
Noel & Gabby

*Celebration on Ice*
Jason & Lauren

*Crushing on Ice*
Brenna & Brendan

*Jump into the future, where the Bevvie Bar is now the Coffee Loft, the set for fun sweet rom coms!*

*That Thing You Brew*
Xavier & Penny

*Turn the page to get the recipes for Quinn's Toasted Almond Peanut Butter Cookies and Brodie's Crispmas Wreaths! For access to more fun series-related recipes, sign up for my newsletter at KerryEvelyn.com*

# Quinn's Toasted Almond Peanut Butter Cookies

**Prep:** 20 min
**Cook:** 15 min
**Cool:** 30 min

## Ingredients

- 1 1/2 cups all-purpose flour
- 1 cup packed brown sugar
- 1 cup granulated sugar
- 1 teaspoon baking powder
- 1/2 teaspoon kosher salt or sea salt
- 3/4 cup unsalted butter, at room temperature
- 1 teaspoon pure vanilla extract
- 2 large eggs
- 1 cup creamy peanut butter
- 2 cups raw whole almonds
- Parchment paper

## Directions

1. Whisk the flour, baking powder, and salt together. Set aside.
2. In a mixer, cream the butter, brown sugar, and granulated sugar for 2-3 minutes until light and fluffy.
3. Beat in the peanut butter until combined.
4. Beat in the eggs and vanilla. Stir in the flour mixture until just combined.
5. Stir in the chopped almonds.
6. Cover and chill the dough for a minimum of 1 hour.
7. Preheat the oven to 375°F.
8. Roast the almonds in a single layer on a baking sheet for 6 minutes or until lightly toasted. Cool until able to handle. Set aside enough to garnish the top of each cookie.
9. Chop the remaining almonds. Set aside.
10. Line 2 sheet pans with parchment paper.
11. Form the dough into 1 1/2-inch balls and place on the pan 2 inches apart. Lightly press a whole almond on top of each dough ball.
12. Bake at 375°F for 11-14 minutes or until the cookies are lightly browned. Transfer to a wire rack to cool.

# Brodie's Crispmas Wreaths

**Prep:** 5 min
**Cook:** 10 min
**Set:** 10 min

## Ingredients

- Parchment paper
- ½ cup butter
- 1 10-ounce package mini marshmallows
- Green liquid food coloring
- ¾ cup white vanilla baking chips
- 5 cups sugar-frosted corn flake cereal
- Red M&M's or cinnamon candies

## Directions

1. Microwave butter uncovered in a large bowl for 30-60 seconds or until melted.

2. Add marshmallows; mix to coat. Microwave uncovered for 60-90 seconds, stirring every 30 seconds, until marshmallows are completely melted and mixture is well blended.
3. Stir in green food coloring to desired shade of green. Add vanilla baking chips to the marshmallow mixture. Stir until melted. Microwave for an additional 30 seconds if necessary.
4. Stir in cereal until evenly coated.
5. Spoon ½-cup-sized dollops of the cereal mixture onto parchment paper. Form into 10-12 wreath shapes and decorate with red candies.
6. Cool in refrigerator for 10 minutes before serving.

*For more recipe cards, additional recipes, bonus epilogues, and printable activities, sign up for Kerry's newsletter at KerryEvelyn.com.*

# Acknowledgments

I'm so super excited to launch this new series! And so super grateful to the VIP readers who are helping to make it extra sweet, fuzzy, and swoony! If you loved reading this story, be sure to thank my Bridie Crew: Andrea Payne, Amanda Kunstman, Amanda Petersen, Frieda J. Downing, Gail Silva, Hannah Smith, Judy Marshall, Katie Carley, Lori Wilen, Sarah Graves, Shanna Johnson, Tabitha Cagle, Tonya Spitler, and Valerie Hills! Your ideas and suggestions are so helpful and funny, and it's been such a pleasure working with you to further develop Palmer City and Brenna's world.

Huge thanks to Noah Kartagener, my brilliant architect friend, for the design and construction details!

Lasairiona McMaster, you rock! Thanks for all the things, all the help, all the love, and all the REAL Cadbury chocolate!

Monica Cobine, thank you so much for reading my books and blessing me with your feedback. It's always on point, and I appreciate you so much.

Candace Colt, I love you bunches and love that we are on this sweet rom journey together. Almost five years together; isn't that crazy? Thanks for keeping me sane (mostly) haha!

Korin!! So much gratitude for your friendship and all that you do! Your love and support is everything to me.

TMACKS & SSCG: Mwaaaaaaaaaaaaaaaah!

BookNookNuts, thanks for always making time for me.

You rock, and I'm so glad you're on board for this new series, too!

Chris Kridler, thank you so much for choosing to work with me again! This new series is going to be so awesome, and I'm so excited to partner with you again!

Anthony, Kailyn, and Nicholas, I love you three more than life itself! Thanks for the time you give me to do what God gave me to do. XOXO!

And last but certainly not least, thanks to God for all of his downloads and making all of this possible. I love our partnership!

# Books by Kerry Evelyn

**Crane's Cove**

*Love on the Edge*

*Love on the Rocks*

*Love on the Beach*

*Love on the Fly*

*Love on the Heart*

*Love on the Brain*

*A Night at the Inn: A Lizzie Borden Short Story*

*The Cotton Candy Caper: A Fall Carnival Story*

*A Night in the Passage: A Crane's Cove Short Story*

*The Fisherman Nutcracker: A Whimsical Christmas Story*

*A Night in the Cabin: A Crane's Cove Short Story*

*A Second Shot at Love: A Second Chance Romance Novelette*

*A Home for Christmas: A Sweet Southern Christmas Story*

**Cat's Paw Cove**

*Moon Mist Manor Book 1: Christmas at Moon Mist Manor*

*Moon Mist Manor Book 2: Love Overrules the Lawyer*

*Moon Mist Manor Book 3 The Beachcomber's Buccaneer Bounty*

## Palmer City Voltage

*Love on the Ice: A Sweet Small-Town Second Chance Hockey Romance Novelette*

*Cruising on Ice: A Sweet Small-Town Friends-to Lovers Hockey Romance*

*Christmas on Ice: A Sweet Small-Town Holiday Hockey Romance*

*Sparks on the Ice: A Sweet Small-Town Christmas Auction Short Story* (Subscriber Bonus)

*Melting the Ice: A Sweet Small-Town Late to Love Hockey Romance*

*Celebration on Ice: A Small-Town Sweet Second Chance Hockey Romance*

*Crushing on Ice: A Sweet Small-Town Fake Dating Hockey Romance*

## The Coffee Loft Series

*That Thing You Brew: A Sweet Small-Town Hockey Rom Com*

## Once Upon Academy

*Birds of a Feather* (Prequel)

*Bird's Eye View* (Once Upon Academy Volume 1)

*Phoenix Rising* (A Once Upon Academy Duet)

## Collections

*Crane's Cove Box Set 1*

*Small-Town Christmas*

*Crane's Cove Chronicles*

**Nonfiction**

*City Nights* (How I Met My Other Anthology)

*Fenway: A Beacon of Hope* (How I Met My Other 2 Anthology)

*The Believer's Journal for Everyday Faith*

*The Advent Experience Keepsake Planner*

*How to Binge-Write Your Novel*

**The Brewer Brides**

*Keep Me in Mind* (Subscriber Bonus)

*One Margarita*

COMING SOON:

*Born to Fly*

*Head Over Boots*

*'Til You Can't*

*Two Pink Lines*

*Goodnight Kiss*

*Make it Sweet*

*Barn Song*

*Nobody But You*

# Crane's Cove

*Sweet small-town romances
with hope, healing, and happily-ever-after.*

Crane's Cove is an idyllic coastal town, set between the Atlantic Ocean and the Acadian Woods. More than half the land has been in the Crane family for generations. Visitors are just as welcome as the many lifelong residents, many of whom are Cranes or are descendants of the Wabenakis, the Native Americans who first lived on this land. Other longtime families came to the area a century ago to work in the whaling, fishing, and shipping industries.

There's always a friendly face waiting to serve customers at quaint eateries, like Dockside Ice Cream, an ice cream parlor shaped like a giant milk bottle, or The Lobster Trap. And the Cliffside Diner is probably the only place where a former FBI agent pours the coffee and slices the pie. A tiny white clapboard church with stained glass and polished pews is the beating heart of the town.

Craggy cliffs descending to beautiful beaches, horseback-riding trails through white birch and pine forests, and secluded wildflower meadows offer gorgeous views that could only be painted by God. Guests can experience horseback rides, ocean kayaking, and midday picnics at the Cliff Walk Resort, which offers luxury suites as well as rustic cabins. Townsfolk mingle with resort guests at beach potlucks and movie-themed nights, complete with karaoke performances by the town's "golden girls." Crane's Light, a floating lighthouse, now converted into an exclusive guest suite, provides the finishing touch to an already perfect town.

## LOVE ON THE EDGE

*A Sweet Small-Town Friends-to-Lovers Bodyguard Romance*

**His colonel hired him to protect her, not to fall in love. But their fake honeymoon at a seaside resort might just save their hearts as well as her life.**

When her life is upended by a vicious stalker, Lanie Owens retreats to a seaside resort where she can heal in peace while the authorities hunt down her stalker. The last thing she wants is to get bossed around by the handsome bodyguard who's been hired to protect her.

Army Ranger Matt Saunders has almost recovered from the injuries he sustained during the hellish event that almost took his life. Anxious to prove he's fit for duty, he accepts the position to protect his former colonel's granddaughter. Their faith, values, and struggles with PTSD draw them together, but is it enough to rearrange their lives?

When Lanie's location is exposed, Matt will do everything

it takes to protect her—and find a way for them to be together.

## LOVE ON THE ROCKS

*A Sweet Small-Town Second Chance Romance*

**Their love surged and crashed like waves in a storm. They'll need to seek shelter in each other to rescue their happily-ever-after.**

Kat Daniels has returned to Crane's Cove with one goal: to put the pieces of her life back together. One of those pieces—the most important one—is Easton Crane. Breaking off their engagement after he stuck by her, supported her, and loved her through the years of her agonizing recovery from a traumatic accident was the biggest mistake she's ever made. It's going to take everything she has to earn his trust again and prove that she's here to stay.

Easton Crane was shattered when Kat left town—and him. Her desertion taught him a valuable lesson he'll never forget —and he won't make the same mistake twice. Running the stables and renovating the lighthouse in the cove into a luxury accommodation for his family's resort have to remain his top priority. She's the only woman he'll ever love, but he'd rather be alone than give her the reins to his heart again.

When his parents rehire Kat to work in the stables, Easton goes out of his way to avoid her. She's got every right to work and board her horse there—but he doesn't have to like it. When a hurricane nearly destroys the barn, Kat's horse is gravely injured. Only Easton has the skills and training to help Mocha, and he'll need Kat's help to save her.

And just maybe, in the process, they'll save each other.

## LOVE ON THE BEACH

*A Sweet Small-Town Friends-to-Lovers Opposites Attract Romance*

**She had big-city dreams with big-city goals. No one was more surprised than she was when she found her place—and her heart —in her small seaside hometown.**

Returning to Crane's Cove for the summer to regroup and reset, Shelby Porter has no time for nonsense. She needs to reassess her career goals and find a way to fund them. There's no room in her life for the too-kind, too-handsome-for-his-own-good, and too-sweet-for-his-tea Georgia transplant who's become besotted with her.

In all the years Detective Damon Saunders lived in Atlanta, the city never seemed like home. During a brief trip to Crane's Cove for a family wedding, he finally understood why. He may hide a haunting past behind his dimpled perma-smile, but the night he met Shelby, he knew what home was supposed to feel like.

When Shelby makes it clear that she's leaving at the end of August, Damon is determined to convince her to stay. She's torn between family obligations and her desire to make a difference in the world.

If he can open her eyes to how much good she can do by staying here, maybe she'll also see what he sees—that their feelings for each other are the forever kind.

## LOVE ON THE FLY

*A Sweet Small-Town Reverse Grumpy-Sunshine Workplace Romance*

**Love was the ultimate risk in a game she didn't want to play.**

Up-and-coming interior designer Caroline Owens doesn't believe in happy endings. After years of disastrous dates and seeing firsthand how love wreaks havoc, she declares a dating detox on the eve of a work event that will make or break her career.

After a yearlong mission trip, pilot JC Crane returns home to Maine for the summer to take on more responsibility at his family's Cliff Walk Resort. Torn between his dreams of running the resort and his calling for mission work, he finds the only clear feelings he has are for Caroline, the woman he couldn't forget after her sister's wedding months ago.

When Caroline books the most important weekend of her career at his family's resort, finding ways to make her smile and rekindle her spark becomes JC's number-one goal. They might be drawn to each other, but neither can figure out how an ambitious businesswoman and a traveling missionary can make a long-distance relationship work.

Their tenuous bond is put to the test when a disaster-relief mission throws JC into danger and forces Caroline to follow her heart. Can she rescue him and their love before it's too late?

## LOVE ON THE HEART

*A Sweet Small-Town Second Chance Christmas Romance*

**She thought he was her soulmate—then he left, crushing her hopes for a future together.**

Molly Crane's divorce was incredibly painful—a pain so deep she's gone to great lengths to protect her heart. But there was something different about the Cliff Walk Resort's spring hire, and she allowed herself to fall for him. Then he left without a word, breaking her heart all over again. Her family and building her event-planning business give her the stability she needs—until Jack returns, shaking her life to its foundation.

Jack Dalton, an executive protection specialist and Special Forces veteran, made a big mistake leaving Molly behind. He has the courage to face any enemy, but telling the full truth about his life to a woman with grief equal to his own scared him. He's finally ready to face his feelings and win her back, unless danger and her own fears get in his way.

Meeting again as the magic of the holidays lights up Crane's Cove, they can't deny their chemistry is as intense as ever. But Jack still has a big secret, and he's already broken her trust once before.

Can they overcome their heartaches to trust in each other and face the future together? Or will pasts—and a terrifying threat from Jack's former life—destroy their love before it has a chance to blossom again?

## LOVE ON THE BRAIN

*A Sweet Small-Town Friends-to-Lovers Medical Romance*

**He was her BFF until life got in the way. Now he's back, right when she needs him most.**

All Jane Porter Allen ever wanted was a big family, front porch, and white picket fence. That dream was laid to rest alongside her husband, Casey, when their life was just getting started. Now, as their son, Noah, faces a similar life-threatening diagnosis, she's forced to confront her past as she struggles with how to save her little boy's future.

Enter Ryan Engstrom, Jane's college bestie and Casey's childhood best friend. A pediatric neurosurgeon, he's full of regrets and determined to help Noah. He'll need to move mountains to make sure Noah receives the best medical treatment possible—all the while fighting his own personal demons as he faces a heart-wrenching decision.

Though still deeply grieving past traumas, Jane and Ryan are just as in tune with each other as ever. When their feelings grow beyond friendship, everything hangs in the balance, including Noah's life. Now, they must confront their pain and make a choice—continue on separate paths and miss out on a second chance at love, or risk everything to find a way to build a future together.

# Cat's Paw Cove Romances

FEATURING FAVORITE CHARACTERS FROM THE
CRANE'S COVE WORLD

Cat's Paw Cove, Florida, is an enchanting seaside town and favorite tourist destination. But there's something unusual about the locals, both human and feline. The popular Shipwreck Museum might just take you back in time, and the historic Sherwood House holds secrets old and new.

Adopt a furever friend at the Cove Cat Café, treat yourself to a psychic reading at Eye of Newt metaphysical shop, pick up a special trinket from Black Cat Antiquities. And don't be surprised if you find your heart in the magic of Cat's Paw Cove.

In the harbor, five islands form the pad and toe beans of a cat's paw. The large island is a protected home to magical and mystical beings, in the care of a family of Native Americans who moved out to the island in the early 1700s. A lighthouse stands guard on the northernmost of the toe bean islands, and the other three are privately owned.

On Guinevere Island, surrounded by an enchanted mist, sits the town's oldest resort. Built in the mid-1800s by Native Americans and British settlers, Moon Mist Manor is a luxury destination unlike any other. Those born on the island and a select few entrusted with the secret can see and hear the beings that have made a home on this sacred land. But visitors beware—unseen forces and intruders are continually battling the island's defenses for a place to call their own ... and its very existence.

## CHRISTMAS AT MOON MIST MANOR

After spending months apart, Matt and Lanie Saunders are delighted to be together again for the holidays. While Matt aided disaster relief efforts across the country, Lanie's dreamed about that white Christmas she wanted for her Southern-born husband. This year, they'll have it all—a Babymoon in Florida and then up to Maine with their families and friends. First stop: Moon Mist Manor in Cat's Paw Cove where Matt spent many magical summers as a boy.

Lanie doesn't quite grasp what makes the island so spellbinding for Matt. She knows she shouldn't be upset when she has him, a baby on the way, new friends, and an enchanting kitten named Pippi to make her spirit bright. But try as she might, she can't shake the resentment that's been festering in her heart.

Just as Lanie makes an eye-opening discovery that puts everything into perspective, she's forced to retreat to the manor's medical suite as a storm rolls through. Matt's outside helping search for runaway Pippi, but he isn't answering his phone. Will he make it back in time to receive the most wonderful Christmas gift of all?

## LOVE OVERRULES THE LAWYER

Once upon a time, Rachel Saunders told Javier Consuelos she was truly, madly, deeply in love with him. And he ran.

Fifteen years later, Javier still regrets breaking Rachel's heart, but watching her succeed as a corporate attorney confirmed he did the right thing. A long way from his troubled childhood, he's cooking for celebrities and giving back to the community that believed in him.

But Rachel has had a tougher fifteen years than she's let on. When she's offered an opportunity to start over, she realizes her dream job will put her in constant contact with Javier. Distraught, Rachel flees to Moon Mist Manor on Guinevere Island to connect with her longtime feline adviser, Ameerah, who has always steered her in the right direction.

When Javier unexpectedly shows up to make amends this Valentine's Day weekend, and with no vacancies in town, the trio are stuck together. That is, until mischievous visitors threaten to overtake the island. Can Rachel and Javier overcome magical forces and their painful past to save the resort and get a second chance at love?

## THE BEACHCOMBER'S BUCCANEER BOUNTY

Former Detective Leda Bellini, AKA Lisa Belmont, has had enough of witness protection. Determined to start a new life on her terms, she shifts into her swan form, ditches her security detail, and heads to Moon Mist manor, a resort island in Cat's Paw Cove, Florida. Somehow, the owner knows her true identity and has been expecting her. Leda is blown away (literally) when she finds herself and a mysterious cat named Davy transported back in time to the year 1717 and into the arms of a pirate with hypnotic emerald eyes. Being trapped in the past may be just the sort of adventure she's been yearning for.

Disgraced Royal Navy Captain Drake Reid misread a command during the Jacobite rebellion that cost him everything. His only shot at redemption is to pose as a pirate and retrieve the magical Avalon roses for the king. Blown off course by a storm, his ship misses St. Augustine where the Spanish are rumored to have brought the priceless treasure. Further complicating the matter is the scandalously underdressed woman who appeared out of nowhere and is now hiding aboard his ship.

Leda finds herself drawn to the enigmatic, Iliad-quoting pirate. On the cusp of achieving his goal, Drake is betrayed, and he and his crew are taken captive. Can Leda recover the Avalon roses before they're executed? Or is their fate already sealed?

# Palmer City Voltage

## A LAST CHANCE HOCKEY ROMANCE SERIES

Make-or-break careers become complicated when these players meet their matches. Talented athletes on the brink of their ultimate goals. Brilliant women with big dreams. With eyes on the prize, will love get in their way or lead them to their happily-ever-afters?

Travel to Palmer City, a quaint little former mining town with a big heart, just outside Colorado Springs where love melts the ice.

### LOVE ON THE ICE

Ginny Perdita has traded in her figure skating costumes for coaching at her home rink after a tragic accident took her sister and brother-in-law, orphaning her young niece and nephew. Thrown into instant parenthood and now unable to compete, she's had to bury her Olympic dreams.

Alexei Kriz is starting over after his girlfriend refused to follow him to Colorado Springs to play hockey. Despite that, he's thrilled to have been picked up for the Palmer City

Voltage and plans to throw himself into the game and volunteer work with the Flying Stars, a youth team of special athletes who also call the rink home. There, he runs into Ginny - the one who got away.

It's been years since Ginny and Alexei first connected back in Sochi. Still frosty that he never called her after the games, Ginny is wary of his intentions and affection for her and the three-year-old twins. Still, she can't ignore the feelings that pull her to the Czech defenseman.

When they're assigned to work together for the Flying Stars program fundraiser, Ginny's ice begins to melt as she watches him guide the young players and dote on the twins. Alexei vows to not let her get away forever this time. When she's offered a high-level coaching job in New York, can he warm her heart for a second chance at love?

## CRUISING ON ICE

Taylor Ranford has three immediate goals: have a blast on her birthday cruise with her sister, help Team USA win the international cheerleading title, and earn enough money to put her through grad school. Not part of the plan: her sister getting sick and sending her best friend—and Taylor's longtime crush—in her place. She can't face the only guy she's ever had feelings for treating her like she's his little sister when she really wants so much more.

After a big blow to his career—and his ego—and with no immediate plans for the next season, Kingston Brewer jumps at the opportunity to go on a last-minute cruise with the bouncy-ponytailed cheerleading coach. Taylor had always been there when he needed her most, and he holds a soft spot for her in his heart. But after a few days on the ship, Kingston begins to see Taylor as more than just his best friend's little sister.

Just when he thinks they can explore a future together, Kingston gets THE call from his agent. Now he has to make one of the most difficult choices in his personal and professional life. Will he give up the professional chance of a lifetime for a chance with the girl he's fallen head-over-skates for?

## CHRISTMAS ON ICE

Stuck in Palmer City, Colorado with a big stack of broken dreams, Kami Spencer picks up a serving job to help make ends meet while she finishes her doctorate. Taking care of her daughter, finishing her degree, and moving back home to South Carolina are her focus, until her plans are complicated by a charming hockey player who skates his way into their lives.

Trask Emerson is at the top of his game. As the Voltage's alternate captain and star defenseman, he's sure to move out of the minors sooner than later. Lately, though, he mostly looks forward to celebrating with the team at Brewski's and getting to know the guarded new server and her little girl. The two have captured his attention and stolen his heart.

The spark between them is undeniable, even if Kami won't admit it. Fate sends them both to Charleston for Christmas, and Trask is determined to show her what a future together could look like. Just when Kami is warming up to the idea of a relationship, tragedy strikes. Trask is there for her, but Kami is afraid to lose her heart again. Can he break down her walls and convince her they belong together?

It just may take a Christmas miracle for them to get their happily-ever-after ...

## MELTING THE ICE

The Voltage's season is off to a rocky start, and no one feels it more than Coach Zander Conway. With his two star players gone, he has to rebuild the team to defend last year's championship. Canadian rookie Noel Allaire may be the missing link, but he's young, inexperienced, and adjusting to being away from home.

Single mom Gemma Allaire's world centered on raising Noel, her eighteen-year-old son and Voltage hockey prodigy. When Noel embarks on a professional career in the States, she follows him without a second thought. In a new town and a new country, Gemma and Noel need a place to live, but she never expected to find a rental next door to her son's handsome and charming head coach.

Neither Gemma nor Zander can resist the magnetic attraction pulling them together. Has the time come for them to open their hearts to love? But after a violent collision on the ice threatens what she holds most dear, ghosts from Gemma's past threaten to destroy their fragile new relationship. Zander is forced to grapple with a decision that could result in losing the woman he can't live without.

## CELEBRATION ON ICE

He messed up big time. And now he's lost the woman who meant everything to him.

Goalie Jason Dexter's very public ultimatum at the team's New Year's Eve party was the dumbest thing he'd ever done. The very public break-up that followed supports that fact.

He should never have demanded that his girlfriend, Lauren, drop her career and everything she's been working for to follow him up to the NHL. Especially not for a team that might send him back to the minors after the season ends.

Instead of celebrating his career achievement of tending goal for a playoff-bound organization, he's mourning the loss of the love of his life.

When the team makes it to the playoffs, Jason gets his chance to make saves on the ice—but can this heartsick netminder make the biggest save of his life off the ice? He'll have to use every skill he's got to convince Lauren he's sorry, and give her the one thing they both need the most—each other.

It's game time. If he can win her back, he'll spend the rest of his life showing her how much he loves her.

## CRUSHING ON ICE

It could be a match penalty for him if he breaks her fake-boyfriend rules...

Brenna Brewer is determined to make her wedding planning business a success. She doesn't have time in her life for a heartthrob hockey player—no matter how sweet, charming, or helpful he is. At her family's sports pub by the arena, she's seen hundreds of players come and go over the years, and at some point, they all get traded and leave. But there's one player she can't stop thinking about, and the fine line at the edge of the friend zone is starting to blur.

Brendan Trotter knows what he wants. The woman he's dreamed about for years is now one of his closest friends. Unfortunately, just when his hockey career lands him in her hometown, she's putting down roots and makes it clear she's not interested in a relationship with someone who could get traded at any time.

To woo a potential client, Brenna urgently needs a date for the wedding event of the summer. Brendan's happy to be her plus-one, especially when the weekend offers him a chance to prove to her how perfect they are for each other. Next season's contracts are expected any day now, and he knows it's his last chance to convince her they belong together.

With everything on the line, Brendan devises a plan to take the shot of a lifetime. But breaking Brenna's number one rule could result in more than a major penalty—it could take him out of the game forever.

# Brewer Brides

SWEET SMALL-TOWN WEDDING ROMANCES WITH
HEART, HUMOR, AND HAPPILY-EVER-AFTER

## ONE MARGARITA

*A Sweet Small-Town Grumpy-Sunshine Christmas Romance*

**His life was perfectly perfect. Until she showed up.**
*A little competition, a dash of mischief, and a smidge of
something sweet won't be the only things brewing this holiday
season.*

Keegan Brewer's life is perfectly fine. He's content with his
perfected daily routine: early mornings dreaming up new craft
beers for his family's restaurant, afternoons managing Brewski's from behind the scenes, and evenings syncing Christmas
songs to the LED light display on and around his tiny caboose
home on his grandparents' ranchland. Sure, it irks him that
his favorite retired hockey player is opening a rival restaurant
across the street, and he'll defend his family's business no
matter what it takes. One thing he knows for sure is that he

wants nothing to do with the bombshell blonde who wants his brewery secrets to make her dad's restaurant a success.

Daughter of a hockey legend, heiress to a billion-dollar sports equipment and fashion empire, and Olympic champion in her own right, Astoria Kubek practically grew up at Brewski's. A lifetime ago, she and the Brewer kids were friends, on and off the ice, playing peewee hockey and pranking the pros. She's been tasked with creating a signature brew to put their new family restaurant on the map. And she wants Keegan's help.

It'll take everything she's got to get the grumpy brewer's attention, never mind his assistance. But the man won't even look at her. Astoria is used to winning, but winning Keegan over becomes more than a job—especially when she discovers the power of his dimples and his adoration of her crazy foster kitten. Making him smile is her new mission, even if her messy life gives him hives. She'll do whatever it takes to bring him true Christmas joy—including unleashing her adorable kitty as a secret weapon.

Together, can they craft a perfect beer and gift each other with the most special Christmas gift of all?

*The Coffee Loft Series*

HAPPILY-EVER-AFTERS, COMING RIGHT UP!

THAT THING YOU BREW

*A Sweet Small-Town Hockey Rom Com*

**Every Denver Edge fan thinks they know superstitious blueliner Xavier Schwann's goal scoring secret—the toffee coffee he drinks before every home game. But the truth is, it's really the barista at Palmer City's local coffee shop that brings him good luck.**

When the Bevvie Bar is bought out by a new coffee chain, fans everywhere go ballistic. But Xavier isn't worried. He'll still visit the shop and maintain appearances. As long as Penny Palmer is the one serving him, his game will be fine.

He's fallen hard for the Renaissance-loving barista who mixes his brew. Her shy smiles and harp playing skills captured his attention—and his heart. But after three years, she's still a mystery. When he learns his inheritance of the family castle in Germany is contingent upon him marrying, he's sure that could be the in he needs to win her heart.

But he's got to hurry.

He's only got until his birthday to get married, or he loses everything.

# About the Author

Kerry's sweet romance novels feature small towns, a touch of the supernatural, and unforgettable charming characters pursuing happily-ever-afters. This international award-winning *NSYNC fanatic is fueled on faith, Dunkin' iced coffee, and a love for people, including her amazing family. Kerry loves (in ever-changing order) books, boybands, cats, hockey, sweet drinks, taking selfies, traveling, and the madness of getting the stories in her head onto the page. Find out more and sign up for her newsletter at KerryEvelyn.com/links.

Website: https://kerryevelyn.com/newsletter/
Reader Group: Facebook.com/groups/CranesCoveCrew
Email: Kerry@KerryEvelyn.com
Spotify: tinyurl.com/KerryEvelynSpotify

f facebook.com/KerryEvelynAuthor
⊙ instagram.com/KerryEvelynBooks
𝕏 x.com/theKerryEvelyn
♪ tiktok.com/@KerryEvelynAuthor
⑫ pinterest.com/KerryEvelynBooks
ⓐ amazon.com/Kerry-Evelyn/e/B077LWTYXJ
g goodreads.com/kerryevelynauthor
BB bookbub.com/authors/kerry-evelyn

www.ingramcontent.com/pod-product-compliance
Lightning Source LLC
Chambersburg PA
CBHW032212170626
46808CB00006B/2433